Other Books by Harriet Steel

Becoming Lola

Salvation

City of Dreams

Following the Dream

The Inspector de Silva Mysteries

Trouble in Nuala

Dark Clouds over Nuala

Offstage in Nuala

Fatal Finds in Nuala

Christmas in Nuala

Short stories

Dancing and other stories

AN INSPECTOR DE SILVA MYSTERY

PASSAGE
FROM NUALA

HARRIET STEEL

MYS
STEEL

Author's Note and Acknowledgements

Welcome to the sixth book in my Inspector de Silva mystery series. Like the earlier ones, this is a self-contained story but, wearing my reader's hat, I usually find that my enjoyment of a series is deepened by reading the books in order and getting to know major characters well. With that in mind, I have included thumbnail sketches of those featuring here who took a major part in previous stories. I have also reprinted this introduction, with apologies to those who have already read it.

Four years ago, I had the great good fortune to visit the island of Sri Lanka, the former Ceylon. I fell in love with the country straight away, awed by its tremendous natural beauty and the charm and friendliness of its people who seem to have recovered extraordinarily well from the tragic civil war between the two main ethnic groups, the Sinhalese and the Tamils. I had been planning to write a detective series for some time and when I came home, I decided to set it in Ceylon in the 1930s, a time when British Colonial rule created interesting contrasts, and sometimes conflicts, with traditional culture. Thus, Inspector Shanti de Silva and his friends were born.

I owe many thanks to everyone who helped with this book. My editor, John Hudspith, was, as usual, invaluable and Jane Dixon Smith designed another excellent cover for me, as well as doing the elegant layout. Praise from the many readers who told me that they enjoyed the previous books in this series and wanted to know what Inspector de Silva and his friends got up to next encouraged me to keep going. Above all, heartfelt thanks go to my husband, Roger, without whose unfailing encouragement and support I might never have reached the end.

Apart from well-known historical figures, all characters in the book are fictitious. Nuala is also fictitious although loosely based on the hill town of Nuwara Eliya. Any mistakes are my own.

Characters who appear regularly in the Inspector de Silva Mysteries

Inspector Shanti de Silva. He began his police career in Ceylon's capital city, Colombo, but, in middle age, he married and accepted a promotion to inspector in charge of the small force in the hill town of Nuala. Likes: a quiet life with his beloved wife; his car; good food; his garden. Dislikes: interference in his work by his British masters; formal occasions.

Sergeant Prasanna. In his mid-twenties, married with a baby daughter, and doing well in his job. Likes: cricket and is exceptionally good at it.

Constable Nadar. A few years younger than Prasanna and less confident. Married with a baby boy. Likes: his food; making toys for his baby son. Dislikes: sleepless nights.

The British:

Jane de Silva. She came to Ceylon as a governess to a wealthy colonial family and met and married de Silva a few years later. A no-nonsense lady with a dry sense of humour. Likes: detective novels, cinema, and dancing. Dislikes: snobbishness.

Archie Clutterbuck. Assistant government agent in Nuala and as such, responsible for administration and keeping law and order in the area. Likes: his Labrador, Darcy; fishing; hunting big game. Dislikes: being argued with; the heat.

Florence Clutterbuck. Archie's wife, a stout, forthright lady. Likes: being queen bee; organising other people. Dislikes: people who don't defer to her at all times.

William Petrie. Government agent for the Central Province and therefore Archie Clutterbuck's boss. A charming exterior hides a steely character. Likes: getting things done. Dislikes: inefficiency.

Lady Caroline Petrie. His wife and a titled lady in her own right. She is a charming and gentle person.

Doctor David Hebden. Doctor for the Nuala area. He travelled widely before ending up in Nuala. Unmarried and hitherto, under his professional shell, rather shy. Likes: cricket. Dislikes: formality.

Emerald Watson. She arrived in Nuala with a touring British theatre company and decided to stay. She's a popular addition to local society, especially where Doctor Hebden is concerned. Her full story is told in *Offstage in Nuala*.

Charlie Frobisher. A junior member of staff in the Colonial Service. A personable young man who is tipped to do well. Likes: sport and climbing mountains.

CHAPTER 1

'Oh Shanti, I feel like a little girl who's been waiting for Christmas, and now it's come!'

Jane put down the letter she'd just read, a broad smile on her face. The postman had delivered it while they were having breakfast. De Silva had told the man at Thomas Cook, the travel agents, that it was to be addressed to Jane.

'I'm so glad you're pleased, my love.'

'Oh, I'm more than pleased. You know how much I've wanted to see Egypt and the pyramids. It's all so exciting.' Her expression clouded. 'But are you quite sure we can afford it, dear? It's the same ship that Florence Clutterbuck went on, and it sounds very grand.'

'If the ship's good enough for Florence, it's good enough for us.'

Jane frowned. 'You know what I mean, dear.'

He reached across the table and patted her hand. 'I do, but there's no need to worry – we can afford to treat ourselves. I have my long-service bonus, remember? And, on top of that, we've never spent much of the money my parents left me.'

'Well, if you're sure, then there's nothing I'd like better.'

A mischievous twinkle came into her eyes. 'I may need some new clothes, though.'

'Naturally. Oh, and I have another surprise.'

'Gracious!'

'Only a little one this time. Wait here.'

He left the room and returned a few moments later carrying a brown leather case the size of half a brick.

'What is it?'

'I'll show you.'

Carefully, he removed the camera from its case. 'I've fancied having one of these for quite a while now, and this seemed the perfect time. It's a Kodak. I bought it from the shop in Hatton. I bought plenty of rolls of film too. I'll be able to take lots of photographs of the places we visit, so we'll remember them perfectly when we come home.'

'That's a marvellous idea.'

'I thought so.'

She hesitated. 'But is it complicated to work?'

'Have you no faith in my abilities? It'll be a slice of cake.'

Jane smiled. 'A piece of cake, dear. Seriously, mightn't it be a good idea to practise a little before you take it on our holiday?'

'I intend to, and we have the perfect occasion coming up.'

'You mean Archie and Florence's annual garden party at the Residence?'

'Yes.'

* * *

The day of the garden party was a little cooler than usual. De Silva was glad of it; he knew from experience that there wasn't a great deal of shade in the Residence's garden.

He and Jane arrived punctually at three o'clock and, once they had said hello to Archie and Florence who were waiting to greet their guests, began to walk around the garden.

'Good afternoon, Mrs de Silva. Inspector de Silva.'

De Silva and Jane turned from admiring a flowerbed to find Charlie Frobisher beaming at them.

'Why, Mr Frobisher,' said Jane. 'How nice to see you. Isn't it a lovely day for a garden party?'

'Indeed it is, Mrs de Silva.'

They chatted for a while until Frobisher saw their mutual boss, Archie Clutterbuck, beckoning him over.

'Will you excuse me? I think duty calls.'

'Of course,' said Jane with a smile.

'What a charming young man,' she remarked as Frobisher walked away.

'Let me guess. You're still plotting a match for him.'

'It does seem a dreadful waste that he's not married. There aren't many eligible bachelors in Nuala.'

She looked around at the crowd of guests. De Silva followed her eyes and saw Archie talking to Emerald Watson and Doctor Hebden – another of Jane's matchmaking targets.

'Jane, people must be allowed to make their own choice. We did.'

'I know, but David Hebden and Emerald do seem a perfect match. Dear Doctor Hebden is prone to be a little too serious, so Emerald would lighten him up. They could play golf together. I believe they both enjoy the game.'

De Silva observed the couple for a moment. David Hebden certainly did look more relaxed than usual. He was listening intently to what Emerald Watson was saying and laughing a lot.

He chuckled. 'I'm glad you have it all worked out, my love. Now that their future is decided, I think I'll get on with taking some photographs. I noticed the regal lilies by the summer house are looking particularly splendid today.'

Jane drifted away to talk to friends and de Silva started to get to grips with the camera. He had already had some practice at Sunnybank, but the Residence gardens were far more extensive and, as well as the pretty summerhouse, had several interesting garden follies.

When he had used up most of the exposures on the film roll, he decided to have a rest from photography and went to watch the young people who had taken up Archie's offer to use the Residence tennis courts. Settled in a patch of shade and a deckchair, he observed the two couples who were playing mixed doubles. Tennis, he reflected, was quite an interesting game, although not one his countrymen had ever much taken to. Their passion was cricket.

'A penny for your thoughts?'

He looked up to see that Jane had joined him.

'Oh, nothing important. I was just enjoying a quiet sit, watching other people run about.'

'Then you won't want to join in the game of rounders Charlie Frobisher is organising for the young people.'

He stood up and went to fetch another deckchair. 'Far too energetic,' he said when he came back with it. 'Anyway, it's a long time since I was a young person.'

Side by side, they sat and watched for a few minutes, the rhythmic thud of racket on ball providing a soothing counterpoint to the drowsy heat of the afternoon.

'Ah, there you are.' Archie Clutterbuck's jovial tones brought them back to the present. Archie shaded his eyes with one hand and scrutinised play. 'I used to be fond of a game of tennis, but too damned hot for me in this country. Golf's more my line.'

He chortled. 'Mixed doubles can be a bit of a blood sport. Many an engagement's been broken over a disputed point.'

De Silva smiled in return. It seemed the appropriate reaction, although he never ceased to wonder at the oddity of the British capacity for taking their sports so seriously. Of course, it was a different matter where cricket was concerned. That was entirely justified.

Florence's dulcet tones reached his ears. She joined them and smiled up at Archie. 'Do you remember all those tennis parties when we were young, dear? Why, I recall we first met at one given by the Frasers.'

'Eh? Oh yes, the Frasers. Lived in Twickenham.'

'Richmond, dear.'

'Had two very pretty daughters.'

Florence sniffed. 'I don't recall them being especially noteworthy.'

Archie tucked her arm in his. 'I expect I'm mistaken. In any case, I only had eyes for you, my dear.'

Jane and de Silva exchanged amused glances. Archie was obviously enjoying his own party.

'Didn't know you were a photography enthusiast, de Silva,' he remarked, looking at the camera case that de Silva had hung over the arm of his deckchair.

'The camera's a recent purchase. I thought it would be useful on our holiday.'

'Ah yes, your cruise. Which ship are you going on?'

'I told you, dear,' interrupted Florence. 'The *Jewel of the East*, the one I sailed on. I'm sure you'll have a marvellous time,' she continued, addressing the de Silvas. 'I hear the Petries will be on board too. They're going home to England on leave, you know.'

'I don't suppose we'll see anything of the Petries on the ship,' remarked de Silva, as the Clutterbucks walked away to talk to some of their other guests. 'They're bound to be in Cabin Class. I'm afraid that was rather too expensive,' he added apologetically.

'I'm not sure I'd want to be there anyway. Too formal, from how Florence described it. No, Tourist Class will suit me very well. I'm sure we'll have a wonderful time.'

Later, as dusk crept on, and the party came to an end, Jane and de Silva returned to the Morris. In the line of departing cars, it edged down the drive and onto the main road. As the traffic jam cleared, de Silva pressed his foot on the accelerator and the needle climbed. He rested his elbow on the sill of the open window and felt a cooling wind. He could almost imagine that they were already on the ocean, enjoying the sea breeze.

CHAPTER 2

Jane gazed up at the sleek, black hull of the Blue Star Line's *Jewel of the East*. The white-painted railings of the decks above gleamed in the sunshine. Three massive black funnels topped off the impressive picture, the two to the fore and aft belching grey smoke into the azure sky.

'The middle funnel is just for show,' de Silva remarked. 'To balance out the ship's silhouette. Magnificent, isn't she?'

He paused and took another photograph. 'She weighs nearly sixty thousand tons,' he went on, 'and she can reach a speed of twenty-two knots in calm seas. I'm afraid though, that we'll have to share her with a lot of other people.'

'You've been doing your homework, dear,' said Jane with a laugh. 'But I'm sure sharing with other people won't be a problem. There looks to be a great deal of room.'

Crowds thronged Colombo's passenger dock: some, like de Silva and Jane, boarding the ship; others waving off passengers, or merely curious to see the *Jewel* at close quarters and watch her put to sea. Not far from where they stood, a gleaming, black Bentley was being hoisted into the hold. De Silva held his breath. Hundreds of pounds worth of remarkable engineering and design hung from those ropes. Covetable as the car was, at that moment, he was glad it didn't belong to him. Fondly, he thought of his beloved Morris, safe in the garage at Sunnybank.

The Bentley swung out of sight and de Silva exhaled.

Further down the quayside, workmen, stripped to their loincloths, laboured under the weight of sides of meat, sacks of flour, coffee and tea, and boxes of vegetables and fruits. Chickens, presumably being taken on board for their eggs or for the table, poked their heads between the slats of wooden crates, making a tremendous racket.

'I've heard that in the old days, some passenger ships even took a dairy cow on board,' said de Silva. 'So that you British could have fresh milk with your tea.'

'You'd need a whole herd of cows now.'

De Silva beckoned to the rickshaw driver who had followed them from their hotel with their luggage. They had stayed in Colombo the previous night after travelling down by train from Nuala. 'I'll wait here with the luggage,' he said to the man. 'You go and find us a couple of porters to take it on board.'

The man nodded and hurried away. De Silva paid off the second rickshaw driver who had driven him and Jane, and they settled down to wait. Luckily, they didn't have to do so for long; the first rickshaw man was soon back with two porters. In what seemed no time at all, they were following their luggage up one of the gangways to the deck where the Tourist Class cabins were situated.

So far, so good, thought de Silva with a modicum of relief. The Hatton representative of the travel agent, Thomas Cook, had repeatedly assured him that everything would run like clockwork, but it would be good to get to their cabin and relax for a while. He hoped it would be a comfortable one. The representative had also promised it would be and added that they were very fortunate.

'The accommodation is excellent. It only became available because two passengers travelling to Aden cancelled their tickets. Due to an outbreak of cholera, the ship won't be making its usual stop there.'

The *Jewel of the East* had set out from Hong Kong and

would end her voyage in England, but the de Silvas were leaving the ship at Port Said. There, they would travel inland to spend time in Cairo and visit the pyramids then come back to Port Said in time to board another ship for the return journey to Colombo.

After the hubbub on the quayside, the cabin provided a peaceful contrast. De Silva was pleased to note that it was far enough away from the public rooms for them to be undisturbed, but not so far as to be inconvenient. It was a good size and comfortably furnished with two capacious armchairs upholstered in flowery chintz, a low table with a neat pile of magazines and leaflets giving information about the ship, and two small tables, one on either side of the double bed. There was no mosquito canopy over it. De Silva presumed one wouldn't be needed at sea, but there was a large wooden ceiling fan with brass fittings.

Daylight came from a porthole, and for night, there were four wall-mounted lights with pale pink shades. One short wall was fitted with cupboards, and a chest of drawers doubled as a dressing table. A small bathroom contained all the necessities, and there was even a little dressing room for de Silva.

Jane clapped her hands. 'It's lovely. I'm sure we'll be very comfortable here.' She opened each of the cupboards. 'And there's plenty of room to put things away.'

De Silva pointed to one of the armchairs. 'Sit down for a moment.'

'Why?'

'Because I want a photo of you in our cabin, all ready to set off on holiday.'

Jane grinned. 'Goodness, dear, at this rate you'll have used up all your films by the time we get to Bombay.'

'Don't worry, I have plenty.'

She settled in the armchair and smiled up at him. 'Will this do?'

'Lovely.'

He peered through the viewfinder and pressed down the shutter. 'Now, let's leave our unpacking for later and go on deck. I want to be there when the ship sails. I'd like to take some photographs of what's going on.'

It took them a few minutes to retrace their steps, but they got lost only once before they found their way outside. The view from the deck presented a very different impression from the one they had received when they were standing on the quayside. Back on land, women in bright saris, and vendors hawking souvenirs, fruit and snacks wove their way like vibrant silk threads through the blacks, fawns and creams of the British in their more restrained clothing. De Silva often thought that it was as if, once the British came out East, the sun leached all the colourful hues from their garments; or perhaps they were never there in the first place.

Distance muted the noise from the quayside; it was overlaid by the buzz of the ship as chains clanked and orders were shouted. The smell of the sea replaced the aromas de Silva usually noticed when he was among crowds – dust, sweat, incense, animals, and the whiff of rancid fat and water from sluggish gullies and drains. The deck jolted under their feet, and a volley of hoots made the air quake. People on shore waved their last farewells as the ship slipped her moorings, and sailors hauled ropes on deck, coiling them into small mountains of hemp.

'We're off!' exclaimed Jane. She squeezed his arm. 'Oh, how exciting!'

Suddenly, de Silva felt the deck tilt a fraction. 'I hope the sea stays calm,' he said dubiously.

'I'm sure it will, dear.'

A bell clanged, and an announcement was relayed over the ship's loudspeaker system asking passengers to come to different parts of the ship to be given a safety briefing.

'There was a notice on the cabin wall about that,' said de

Silva. 'We have to take our lifejackets.' He closed his camera case. 'We'd better go back to the cabin and find them.'

Having located the lifejackets on the top shelf of one of their cupboards, they found their way to their designated lounge and listened while one of the ship's officers explained the safety drill.

'I hope we won't need to do this for real,' muttered de Silva as he untangled straps and puzzled over how to fasten them. 'Ah, I have it now.' He helped Jane with hers and stood back. 'Does it suit me?'

'That's hardly the point, dear.'

He grinned. 'I'll take that as a "no". If it saves my life, I suppose it's ungrateful to mind about looking like an oversized orange.'

The briefing completed, they had just returned the lifejackets to their cabin, when another bell rang, and the speaker system announced that tea was being served.

'And if Florence is right,' said Jane, 'it will be a splendid one. Then in a flash, it will be time for dinner. We'll have to walk round the deck at least twice a day if we aren't to get horribly fat.'

'Whatever you say, my love.' He offered her his arm. 'Shall we go?'

CHAPTER 3

Tea was indeed a splendid meal, served in a spacious lounge, one of the two reserved for the use of Tourist Class passengers. White pilasters divided the walls into bays that were painted pale caramel. The floor was covered with a darker coloured linoleum that was pleasantly springy and quiet to walk on; a good choice when the room was so full of people. The chairs were upholstered in brown plush. Crisp white cloths covered the tables and the cups and plates were of fine bone china. Large windows provided a panoramic view of the sea.

Studying the long table where the food was laid out, de Silva decided to forgo the sandwiches, those insipid British creations he had always disapproved of, but the arrangements of cakes and pastries on the multi-tiered china stands looked very tempting. He put a jam puff on his plate then debated whether to choose a slice of fruit cake or a meringue. Jane raised an eyebrow. 'I think we had better make it three times round the deck, dear.'

They found a free table and sat down. Soon, a steward hurried over bringing a pot of tea. Jane allowed a few moments for the tea to brew then poured them both out a cup. As she added milk to hers from the jug already on the table, de Silva reached for the sugar tongs, and she gave him a look of admonishment.

'Only one lump,' he said with a grin.

'I wonder if we'll meet many of the other passengers,' she mused as they ate.

'I expect so. There's certainly no shortage of people, and we're likely to have to share a table at dinner sometimes. You won't mind that, will you?'

'Not at all.'

Tea over, they returned to their cabin. While Jane unpacked into drawers and cupboards, he sat in one of the armchairs and leafed through the information on the table.

'Anything interesting?' asked Jane.

'It says here there'll be dancing to a band after dinner, with a singer called Harry Delaney.'

'What fun.'

She held up the dress she had just unpacked. 'Do you think this will do?'

'Very much so.'

'Goodness! Look at the time. I didn't realise it was so late. We must hurry and get changed. Isn't there a drinks reception in the lounge to welcome new passengers?'

'I believe there is.'

Half an hour later, Jane gave a final pat to her hair and retouched her lipstick. Her dress was midnight blue with a fitted bodice set off by a white collar. The gored skirt fitted smoothly over her hips then fluttered out to a wide hem just above her ankles. A narrow belt made from the same fabric and ornamented with a diamanté buckle emphasised her neat waist.

De Silva, who had been ready for some time, stood up from the armchair where he had been sitting and offered her his arm. 'You look beautiful,' he said. 'You'll outshine every woman there.'

'I'm not sure about that, but thank you, dear.'

They locked their cabin door behind them and set off. As he was on holiday, de Silva had decided to wear the local dress he was most comfortable in. His cream trousers were neatly pressed, and a row of shiny gilt buttons marched down the front of his red, tunic-style jacket.

But as they neared the lounge, and he heard the hum of conversation and laughter swell, misgivings crept into his mind. Perhaps he should have worn western clothes; he might have blended in a little more. Ruefully, he reflected that it was too late now. Jane would tell him not to be silly if he suggested going back to change.

Despite a few raised eyebrows when he and Jane first came to Nuala, they had, for some time, been accepted by most of the members of the town's small society. He gave Jane the credit for smoothing their path with the British community. Her friendly, capable nature and willingness to offer her time and talents to any enterprise had made her popular. As for those who continued to disapprove of a marriage between an Englishwoman and a Ceylonese man, they had mostly learnt to keep their opinions to themselves. Life on board ship, however, was likely to be a different matter. He and Jane would have to begin all over again. Who knew what animosity they might face? He was prepared to put up with it, but he didn't want Jane's holiday marred.

As if she read his mind, Jane gave his arm a reassuring squeeze. Had his footsteps lagged? Assuming a determined smile, he quickened his pace.

The double doors to the lounge were wide open; a smartly turned-out steward wished them good evening and ushered them through. Another steward bearing a silver tray offered wine. Out of politeness, de Silva took a glass, although he wasn't keen on the taste and would have preferred a whisky or an Elephant ginger beer.

'You don't have to drink it, dear,' whispered Jane. 'I'm sure we can find you something else later.'

Under the glitter of the thousands of candle lamps set in the electric chandeliers, the lounge looked more glamorous than it had done in daylight. The tables and chairs had been pulled back around the walls. Now that the space in the middle was exposed, de Silva saw that the linoleum didn't cover the whole floor; a large square area in the middle was, in effect, a wooden dance floor. At the far end of it, a low stage had been set up. Presumably this was where Harry Delaney and the band would be.

'If this is Tourist Class,' murmured Jane. 'I can't imagine what there can be in Cabin Class to surpass it.'

They found a place to sit and watch the other passengers. Not all of them were European. De Silva felt some of his confidence return. Perhaps dinner wouldn't be quite the ordeal he had feared.

When it was time to go to the dining room, they found their names on the large board displaying the table plans and went to sit down. The couple already at the table were British. They introduced themselves as James and Barbara Ross, and conversation flowed easily. They had been on the ship since the beginning of the voyage and were returning to England after five years in Hong Kong.

'That wasn't too bad, was it?' asked Jane as they returned to the lounge for the dancing.

'Oh dear, was it so obvious I was apprehensive?'

'Not to anyone else, I expect.'

He grinned. 'But you know me too well. And no, it wasn't. Mr and Mrs Ross were very pleasant company.'

In the lounge, the band was playing softly. Soon, however, they turned up the volume and launched into *Puttin' on the Ritz*. It was one of de Silva's and Jane's favourites, so they got up to dance. Several other songs they knew well followed.

'Would you like to sit down?' asked Jane, raising her voice to be heard as the last notes of *On a Steamer Coming Over* died away.

'If you would.'

'A cold drink might be nice.'

De Silva fetched them both a lemonade from the bar, and they sat down to watch the dancing and listen to the music.

'Harry Delaney's such a handsome man,' remarked Jane, tapping her foot to the next song. 'Those dark eyes and such an irresistible smile.'

'The American singer?'

She nodded. 'He reminds me of Clark Gable.'

'Very overrated, Clark Gable.'

Jane gave him a teasing smile. 'I do believe you're jealous.'

'I strongly disapprove of any man who turns your head.'

She laughed. 'You've no need to worry, dear.'

'I'm relieved to hear it.'

Just as they had finished their drinks and were about to go back on the dance floor, Harry Delaney announced that he and the band were taking a short break.

'Never mind,' said Jane. 'Why don't we go on deck for a few minutes? It would be lovely to see the stars.'

'Are you sure you won't be cold?'

'I have my wrap if it's chilly.'

There were very few other people outside. A light breeze stirred a string of bunting left over from the ship's departure from Colombo. All the deckchairs had been stacked under canvas for the night and the deck games put away somewhere. Jane snuggled into her wrap, glad of its warmth.

They strolled until they reached the bow of the ship then stopped to lean on the rail and admire the view. In every direction, the dark ocean stretched as far as the eye could see. The moon hung low on the horizon; stars glittered fiercely in the velvet sky.

Strange, thought de Silva, how some sounds were magnified at night. During the day, he'd barely been aware of it, but in the darkness, the slap of waves against the hull was louder and the throb of the ship as she carved her way through the water more insistent. He had a powerful sensation of how small they were compared to the vastness of this alien, watery world, and a shiver went through him.

'Are you feeling cold, dear?' asked Jane.

'It's a bit breezy.'

'Let's go in. The dancing will probably start again soon.'

They were about to walk back when Jane paused. De Silva followed her gaze and noticed that between them and the door that led back to the Tourist Class lounge, a man and a woman stood close together in the shadows by one of the deck chair stacks. The darkness made it hard to see their faces, but both were tall and the woman slender. All at once, there was a flare of orange light, and de Silva caught a glimpse of them in profile. Then the shadows returned, leaving only the glowing red pinpricks of two cigarette tips.

De Silva prided himself that his strong sense of smell enabled him to recognise most of the brands of cigarette that people smoked, but for the moment, the name of this one eluded him. The woman seemed to dominate the conversation now, but then the man cut in, and they appeared to be arguing.

'Let's go around the other way,' whispered Jane. 'We don't want to embarrass them.'

Quietly, they made their way back to the bow and walked down the other side of the deck. When they came back within sight of the place where they had seen the couple arguing, the deck was deserted.

CHAPTER 4

In two days, the ship was due to call at Bombay, before turning westwards towards the coast of Africa. As the port of Aden was closed to them, the stop at Bombay would be longer than usual to take on extra supplies. De Silva was relieved that, although there was a swell, he soon got his sea legs. Between attempting to master the intricacies of deck quoits and shuffleboard, he and Jane relaxed on deck, chatting and reading, or amusing themselves with watching other passengers, many of whom clearly relished having stewards at their beck and call.

Despite Jane's teasing, de Silva used up a second roll of film. Before they left Nuala, he had looked through some of the film and fashion magazines she enjoyed, and he was keen to try out the artistic effects that the photographs there had given him ideas for.

'I shall be the Cecil Beaton of Ceylon, you'll see,' he joked.

He studied a group of young people playing deck quoits. One of the girls wore a halter-necked top and smart linen culottes. A pair of sunglasses with striking, geometrically patterned black and white frames completed her sporty look. 'That's a very fashionable outfit,' he said.

'Goodness, dear, you don't usually take an interest in fashion.'

'Ah, but now I am a photographer, I notice many more things.'

They also took their constitutional strolls around the ship. From the starboard rail, they could just make out India's Malabar Coast, a thin, shimmering line between the sea and the sky.

'The wettest place in India,' said Jane. 'The mountain range of the Western Ghats forms a barrier, trapping the monsoon rains that blow in from the south-west.'

'Indeed it is,' said de Silva, 'I'm glad we aren't stopping there. We have enough rain of our own at home in the monsoon season.'

At dinner on the second evening, they met up with the Rosses again and discovered that James Ross was a keen photographer.

'I didn't venture too many opinions,' said de Silva to Jane after Ross had expanded at length on the cameras he had owned. 'I'm afraid my ignorance would quickly have been unmasked.'

'Never mind, dear. Nice as he is, I'm very glad you don't know as much about cameras as James Ross. I might have to gag you sometimes.'

De Silva chuckled. 'His wife did have a rather resigned expression on her face.'

'As well she might.'

'It could be worse. At least he didn't want to regale me with stories of crimes he's been the victim of and what he thinks about the shortcomings of the policemen dealing with them, as some people do the moment they discover I'm a police inspector.'

'That is some consolation.'

'What he was saying about the official photographer on board was interesting though. If Ross has made friends with him and managed to get the fellow to develop some of his films, I might ask if he can slip something in for me. Normally, I wouldn't mind waiting till we're home, but as this is my first effort, I'm anxious to know how the photographs have come out.'

* * *

After the restful days on the ship, Bombay was an explosion of colour and noise. The waterfront, dominated by the magnificent arch of the Gateway to India, teemed with activity. No sooner had the ship docked and rolled out her gangways than swarms of beggars and vendors buzzed around her.

Jane watched with consternation from the rail. 'Oh dear, I would have liked to go ashore. I've never seen Bombay, but it looks so busy.'

'We have the rest of the day here,' said de Silva. 'We can wait awhile until our presence is less of a novelty. Perhaps it will be quieter in an hour or so.'

An hour later, the knots of beggars and vendors had thinned as he'd hoped. They fetched de Silva's camera and Jane's parasol from the cabin and set off.

The rickshaw they hired drove them along broad streets lined with splendid buildings that rose from the ground like cliffs of stone and glass. Many of the frontages were highly ornate. Government buildings, banks and headquarters of great corporations, they were the palaces of industry and power, as grand as many of the royal residences built by the old maharajahs.

So many things cried out to be photographed that de Silva was very glad he had put a new film in his camera before they set out. He noted with interest that there were many more motor cars than one would see in Colombo. Bombay was a far richer and more populous city than Ceylon's capital. All the trams were double-deckers too; in Colombo they were mainly single-deckers. But, even in this most modern of cities, bullock carts still lumbered, unconcerned, between the vehicles.

'I'd love to see the main bazaar,' said Jane.

De Silva leant forward and tapped the rickshaw man on

21

the shoulder. 'Take us to the bazaar,' he shouted. The man nodded.

Once they were out of the shade of the rickshaw's canopy, the heat intensified. Jane put up her parasol and they set off into the crowds that swirled between the stalls. The hot air was filled with aromas battling for supremacy: spices, herbs, incense and flowers were pleasant to smell. Less attractive odours came from stalls selling tallow candles, kerosene, oily ghee or raw meat.

Jane stopped at a stall selling second-hand books, their pages limp in the moist heat. De Silva shook his head. 'We already have enough with us to start a shop of our own.'

'You're exaggerating, dear. But I suppose there's always the ship's library if we run out.'

She pointed to something behind him. 'That looks intriguing. Shall we go and see?'

De Silva turned to see a man sat cross-legged on a piece of sackcloth laid on the ground. A small brown bird sat on his shoulder. A considerable audience had gathered to watch as the little creature took a thin cigarette from between his fingers, fluttered to his other shoulder and gently put the cigarette in his mouth. He gave the bird a morsel of bread, removed the cigarette from his mouth and began the process again.

Bored after a while, the audience started to drift away, but then the man changed his show. Scattering a handful of coloured beads on the sackcloth, he held out a needle to the bird. It was threaded with red cotton. The bird jerked its head from one side to the other, its bright eyes fixed on the needle, then darted to take it in its beak. Everyone watched as it deftly pushed the needle through the hole in the first bead and tilted it so that the bead ran down the cotton thread. The clapping and laughter resumed as bead after bead was threaded by the same means.

'Clever little thing,' remarked de Silva. He paused to take a photograph. 'I hope he treats it well.'

'I do too,' said Jane. She looked away, her attention distracted. 'Why, I'm sure that's Harry Delaney from the ship. He seems to be in a great hurry. I wonder where he's going.'

'Perhaps like us he just wants to see the bazaar,' said de Silva with a shrug.

'Rushing along at that speed, he won't see much. And if he's not careful, he'll cause an accident.'

Just as she said the words, there was a shout. In his haste, Delaney had barged into a cow browsing at a vegetable stall. The beast lowered its head and pinned him against the wooden side, its tail swishing. Desperately, Delaney struggled to push it away.

Jane's hand went to her mouth. 'Oh dear, I don't expect any of these people will want to drive the cow off. Shanti, shouldn't we do something? The poor man might be badly hurt.'

'Don't worry; I'll go and help him.' But he had only taken a few steps towards the stall when the cow lost interest in its victim and returned to browsing. Delaney didn't wait for a second chance and disappeared into the crowd.

'He was lucky,' said de Silva, returning to Jane. He glanced at his watch. 'Unless you're feeling too hot and would prefer to return to the ship, I'd like to take a few more photographs.'

'I'm happy to stay for a while. As long as you promise not to make us late for dinner.'

'I wouldn't dream of it.'

He looked around and gestured to a street leading away from the bazaar. 'Shall we try going that way? There looks to be an interesting old house on the corner.'

'Whatever you say, dear.'

The street was an attractive one, lined with houses and small hotels, many painted in bright ochres and reds. Here and there, courtyards, cooled by fountains and luxuriant plants, led off it. They all made charming subjects for de Silva's photographs.

But after a while, the buildings became rundown and the pretty courtyards vanished. At a tenement offering rooms to rent by the hour, they decided to turn back.

Later, when they arrived back at the ship, more stores were being taken aboard. It amazed de Silva that so many provisions were needed, but of course, this was now the last time they would dock until they reached Port Said.

While Jane went to their cabin to rest, he strolled along to the lounge. Before they went out, he had noticed bundles of newspapers being delivered. There was plenty of time before he needed to dress for dinner. He would use it to catch up with what was going on in the world. Soon, he was ensconced behind a copy of *The Times of India*.

CHAPTER 5

The ship turned westwards; the next sighting of land would be the coast of Africa. More than a thousand miles of sea to cross! De Silva had never experienced anything like it before. So far, there'd been very little choppy water, but if that changed, he hoped that his newly acquired sea legs wouldn't desert him.

It was just after breakfast on the second morning that there was a knock at their cabin door. He called out, and a steward entered.

'A note for you, sir. Shall I come back later for the reply?'

'Please do.'

He turned to Jane. 'Were we expecting anything?'

'No, and I don't recognise the writing.' She slit open the envelope and pulled out the sheet of notepaper inside. It was thick and creamy and embossed with a crest.

'Oh! It's from Lady Caroline Petrie. She begs us to forgive her for not writing before, and for the short notice. She says she and Mr Petrie would be delighted if we'd join them for dinner this evening.'

De Silva's stomach gave a lurch. He knew Lady Caroline regarded him with favour for his successes at home in Nuala, but dinner with the superior of his boss, Archie Clutterbuck, was a daunting prospect. Cabin Class was bound to be extremely formal. Then he saw Jane's expression. He hated to disappoint her.

She put down the letter. 'We can make an excuse if you don't want to go, dear.'

'But you'd like it if we did, wouldn't you?'

'Well, it's very kind of them to invite us, and I'm sure it will be a lovely evening.'

He swallowed his doubts; it was a small sacrifice to make. 'Then we'll accept. You'd better write a reply before the steward comes back.'

* * *

Lady Caroline had suggested they meet in the foyer that led to the Cabin Class dining room. Its walls were panelled with wood that had a warm, golden sheen, setting off the inlays of stylised fruits and flowers. A domed ceiling decorated with coloured glass reminded him of the entrance hall to Nuala's grandest hotel, The Crown.

'Good evening to you both!'

De Silva and Jane turned to see William Petrie and Lady Caroline smiling at them. Petrie kissed Jane's hand and shook de Silva's. De Silva remembered in time that he should kiss Lady Caroline's hand.

She smiled. 'I'm so glad you were able to join us. I would have sent the invitation sooner, but unfortunately, after the first night out from Colombo, I was unwell.'

'I'm very sorry to hear it, Lady Caroline,' said Jane. 'I trust you're fully recovered.'

'Completely, thank you. Luckily for William, he never suffers from seasickness, but he has been very patient with me.'

A commotion at the door heralded the arrival of a dumpy lady whose grey hair was crimped into tight waves. She wore a black dress, liberally adorned with jet bugle-beads. Despite the warm evening, she had added a heavy

26

fur stole, and numerous ropes of pearls festooned her large bosom. She was rummaging in the small, beaded handbag she carried over her arm. Clearly, she didn't find what she wanted for her thickly powdered face radiated displeasure. She snapped her fingers and a nearby steward jumped to attention.

'Go to Mrs Meadows' cabin and tell her she's forgotten my lorgnette,' she said in a voice that carried far. 'I must have it straight away. Well, what are you waiting for, man? Don't you understand English?'

De Silva heard Lady Caroline murmur something that sounded like, "Oh dear".

The dumpy lady spied them, and the scowl was replaced by an ingratiating smile. She waddled over. '*Dear* Lady Caroline, and Mr Petrie. How delightful.' She extended a hand for William Petrie to kiss. The fingers were swollen and mottled, like uncooked sausages and beringed with diamonds, one the size of a bee-eater's egg.

'Good evening, Mrs Pilkington,' said Petrie.

Ignoring de Silva and Jane, Mrs Pilkington rattled on. 'I'm delighted to see you looking so well, Lady Caroline. I've been *so* looking forward to having the pleasure of your and Mr Petrie's company after we dined at the captain's table that first night. What a pity you've been unable to join us again. I suppose you didn't like to leave Lady Caroline, Mr Petrie.'

'I admit I was concerned for her, but I'm afraid I probably wasn't much help.'

'I *do* hope you called the doctor. Seasickness can be very unpleasant, you know. I used to suffer terribly myself when I was young, but no longer. My doctor in London – a Harley Street man, of course – prescribed some marvellous pills before I left England. You really must consult him next time you travel. I'd be delighted to introduce you.'

'You're too kind,' said Lady Caroline giving Mrs

Pilkington one of her gentle smiles. 'As for the captain's table, we'll have to wait until tomorrow to enjoy your company. We have guests this evening, so my husband has booked a separate one for us.'

For the first time, Mrs Pilkington turned her attention to de Silva and Jane.

'May I introduce Inspector Shanti de Silva and his wife Jane,' said Lady Caroline. 'They are friends from Ceylon. By a happy accident, we find ourselves fellow travellers.'

Mrs Pilkington cast her eye over the de Silvas as if she was inspecting a dish of food that wasn't to her taste. 'Charmed, I'm sure,' she murmured after a palpable interval.

She turned back to the Petries. 'I hope you'll come and have drinks with me in my stateroom one of these evenings. I can promise you French champagne. I always bring my own supply. I never trust what these people give one on board, *even* in Cabin Class. Or perhaps you prefer whisky or brandy, Mr Petrie?'

'In your company, Mrs Pilkington, anything would be a pleasure.'

Mrs Pilkington simpered. 'You flatter me, you naughty man!'

The steward hovered with the retrieved lorgnette. After a few more pleasantries, they parted company with Mrs Pilkington and headed for the dining room.

'I must apologise for her rudeness,' said Lady Caroline quietly as they walked in. 'I'm afraid she isn't quite the lady she likes to think she is.'

'There's no need to apologise, Lady Caroline.'

'Oh, but there is – all the same, it's good of you to say so. Now, let's find our table and enjoy the evening.'

At the top of the dining room's magnificent staircase, de Silva couldn't help pausing to admire the sight before him. A serpentine balcony ran from either side of the staircase right around the walls providing space for tables whose occupants could survey the rest of the diners on the floor below. As in the foyer, the walls were panelled with richly coloured wood. It contrasted with the smart black paint of the balcony's intricate, wrought-iron balustrade. Massive ebony and gold columns supported the domed ceiling, fanning out like palm trees where they met it. The room sparkled with the light of many huge chandeliers. De Silva estimated that each of them must be at least eight feet in diameter.

Descending the sweeping staircase seemed to take a very long time. Despite what de Silva had said to Lady Caroline, it was hard not to be discomfited by Mrs Pilkington. His collar felt tighter than it had when he fastened it in the cabin. As they followed the steward to their table, his feet seemed to mire themselves in the thick, claret-coloured carpet. Thankfully, they turned out to be seated at a reasonable distance from Mrs Pilkington. She had now taken her place between the captain and an elderly gentleman whose dinner jacket blazed with medals.

'Poor things,' remarked Lady Caroline, glancing across the room. 'They're in for a dull evening, I fear. I doubt Mrs Pilkington will let them get a word in edgeways.'

Petrie sent her a quelling look.

'Oh, I doubt she'll hear me,' said his wife airily. 'Do you recognise any of her victims?'

De Silva was shocked. He wasn't used to hearing the British being so outspoken about their fellow countrymen. Lady Caroline was far more of a rebel than she'd appeared to be on previous acquaintance, but then again, she was the daughter of an earl.

A new couple arrived at the captain's table. De Silva noticed that numerous heads turned to admire the glamorous lady. She was tall and willowy, with dark hair worn in a short, stylish cut, bow lips painted crimson, and elegantly arched eyebrows. Her off-the-shoulder gown was made of black velvet, ornamented with a striking diamond brooch in the shape of a fan. She also wore several diamond bracelets.

Her companion was a tall, thin man with protruding eyes, beetling brows, and a rather weak chin. His noticeably long arms hung awkwardly at his sides, giving him a faintly simian air. Even at a distance, de Silva heard his braying laugh as he replied to some remark of Mrs Pilkington's.

'Ah,' said Lady Caroline. 'Diana March and her fiancé, Arthur Chiltern. Sparks may fly with Mrs Pilkington.'

Her husband shot her a reproving look. 'You're very indiscreet this evening, my dear.'

Her blue eyes twinkled. 'We're among friends, William.'

'It's very kind of you to say so, Lady Caroline,' said Jane.

'Not at all.'

Petrie picked up the wine list. 'I must admit, they seem an unlikely couple to me, Chiltern and Mrs March.'

'Yes,' said Lady Caroline. 'One can't help wondering what she sees in him. We sat with them at the captain's table on the first night, and she seems to be a charming, intelligent woman.' She lowered her voice. 'I'm afraid Chiltern is a terrible bore.'

Somewhat firmly, as if he had decided it was time to put an end to the topic of conversation, Petrie put down the wine list. 'I think a dry sherry will go well with the soup. What do you say, de Silva?'

'I'm no expert, sir. I'll be only too happy to follow your advice.'

'Then sherry it is.' Petrie clicked his fingers to summon a passing steward.

'I hope you don't mind my asking, Lady Caroline,' said Jane when he had gone to fetch the sherry. 'But why did you say sparks might fly with Mrs Pilkington?'

'Ah, that's because she and Arthur Chiltern's mother are at daggers drawn over who's the queen of London host-esses. Mrs Pilkington thinks she has the right to the crown, and Lady Chiltern vehemently disagrees. It may be in Mrs Pilkington's mind that she needs to seize her opportunity early and impress on Arthur Chiltern's wife-to-be that she would be wise to defer to her, even if her future mother-in-law doesn't choose to.'

'Caroline, dear, you're very critical tonight.' Petrie's tone was reproachful, but he smiled.

'I wonder what Diana March and Lady Chiltern will make of each other,' he went on. 'I have to admit, I'm rather surprised Arthur took the step of getting engaged without his mother's sanction. But I remember Sir Roger Chiltern, his father, telling me when we once met in England that he was sending Arthur out to work in the Hong Kong branch of the family bank in the hope it would put a bit of backbone into him. He was concerned his son needed to be more independent. Perhaps the experiment has been a success.'

'I do hope the two of them get on,' said Lady Caroline. 'Family life can be very troublesome at the best of times, and Mrs March has already had enough sorrow. A tragedy to be widowed so young. She can't be much more than thirty now. She told me her late husband died a few years ago. Apparently, he was much older than her. Afterwards, she went to live with close friends in Hong Kong. She and Arthur Chiltern met there and became engaged.'

Glasses of nutty, dry sherry were produced, and the soup served. Courses of fish, meat, savouries and dessert followed. Even though British food wasn't often to his liking, de Silva had to admit that it was all very tasty. The Petries were charming company too. He was glad to see Jane's evident pleasure in the occasion.

The hum of conversation, discreet at first, rose as the evening went on. The guests at one of the tables to their left appeared particularly bent on enjoying their evening to the full. As the number of wine bottles set among the debris of their meal mounted, so did their laughter.

Only one of the men was quieter than the rest. He looked about forty with a face that might have been handsome if the ice-blue eyes and the curl of the lip hadn't lent it a reptilian air. Lazily, he surveyed his companions, from time to time contributing to the conversation a remark that made them roar with even louder laughter than before.

'I see Charles Pashley's joined the younger set this evening,' said Petrie dryly.

'Oh dear, I hope they aren't being too indiscreet.' Lady Caroline's smile was impish.

'Charles Pashley's a writer,' Petrie explained. 'He's the author of a few novels, but he writes mainly for the newspapers as a gossip columnist. Some people call him the wittiest man in London, but he has a sharp tongue. If one doesn't want one's private business discussed and lampooned all over town, it's wise to keep well clear of him.'

'I don't suppose the young people would mind that too much, but I expect their parents would see the matter differently,' added Lady Caroline.

A well-stocked cheeseboard arrived, and when that had been cleared away, the waiter brought coffee served in delicate cups and saucers patterned with red and gold Chinese dragons. As he drank his, de Silva thought about the young people's behaviour. Perhaps it was accounted for by their wealth and privilege, but it was not something he had noticed among the young people of his own country. He wondered whether those young Britishers would abandon their frivolity when it was their turn to take up the reins of Empire, or would they turn out to be part of a new world where the great edifice started to crumble?

A world without the Empire: it was hard to imagine it. He'd known nothing but British rule in his country, so had his father and mother. He wished, as he had on many previous occasions, that he had talked more to his father about his views on Ceylon's British masters. Was such a regret something many people experienced as they grew older themselves? This feeling that one had lost a store of knowledge and opinion that would remain forever a mystery? When he was young, he had respected his parents, but also longed to leave home and stand on his own feet. Now he had reached a time in his life when he was inclined to look back and wish he had not been so impatient.

He turned his attention back to the conversation, relieved to find that his moment of distraction had not been noticed. Jane and the Petries were chatting about England and the Petries' plans when they arrived there.

The meal ended and there was dancing. Not in a lounge cleared for the occasion as in Tourist Class but in a proper ballroom, where gilt-framed mirrors reflected the panorama of whirling couples. Breathless, de Silva and Jane sat out after a few dances to watch.

'I'm glad the sea's calm this evening,' said Jane. 'I feel giddy enough as it is.'

He grinned. 'We're not used to having to share the floor with so many other dancers. It tests one's skill when one has to avoid colliding with moving objects.'

Jane leant closer. 'When you get to know them,' she whispered, 'the Petries aren't quite what I expected, particularly Lady Caroline.' She paused, watching them as they glided around the dance floor. 'William Petrie's nimble on his feet for a tall man too. I enjoyed our dance.'

'You're right. Neither of them appears to be too badly afflicted by the British stiff chin.'

Jane gave him a little punch in the ribs. 'You know perfectly well that the correct expression is "stiff upper lip".'

He chuckled. 'Yes.'

'I hope you didn't tread on Lady Caroline's toes when you danced with her.'

'Certainly not.'

One o'clock struck before the orchestra played the last

dance. When it was over, de Silva and Jane thanked their hosts and headed to their cabin. 'What a lovely evening,' said Jane as she sat at the dressing table, brushing out her hair.

De Silva yawned. 'But a very late one. I expect I shall sleep in.'

'Why not? We've nothing to hurry up for.'

He put a hand on her shoulder and she reached up and squeezed it. 'Thank you again, dear. It was such a marvellous idea to come on this cruise. I'll always remember it.'

'I'm glad you're happy. I know, why don't we put out a note telling the steward to serve us breakfast in here?'

'Wonderful.'

'Is half past nine too late?'

'I don't think so.'

'Excellent. I'll do it now.'

Soon, de Silva slipped into a deep sleep. He would probably have stayed there until breakfast arrived, but the sun hadn't long been up when there was an insistent knocking at their cabin door. He opened a bleary eye. 'What's this about?' he muttered. 'Can't that steward read?'

The knocking continued, and Jane stirred. 'Shanti? What's going on?'

'Don't worry. I'll see to it.'

Reluctantly, he climbed out of bed, pulled on his dressing gown and went to the door. He opened it a crack and frowned at the uniformed ship's officer standing outside. Then something in the man's face shook away the remains of de Silva's drowsiness.

'I'm sorry to disturb you, sir,' the officer said solemnly. 'I have a message for you from Mr William Petrie.'

De Silva took the envelope the officer held out to him and opened it; the note inside it read: *My apologies for the interruption to your holiday, but your professional assistance is needed immediately.*

'Where is Mr Petrie?' de Silva asked, folding the note and replacing it in the envelope.

'With Captain McDowell, sir. Shall I wait and show you the way?'

De Silva frowned. 'What's going on?'

'I'm not at liberty to say, sir. I was just instructed to fetch you.'

'Oh, very well. I'll get dressed.'

He closed the door and went to find some clothes.

Jane sat up in bed. 'What is it, dear?'

'I don't know, but it sounds serious.'

She sighed. 'And everything was going so well.'

'I know.'

He finished buttoning the shirt he had hastily found and pulled on a pair of trousers.

'Shanti! That shirt won't do, it's waiting to go to the laundry.'

'If whatever this is warrants dragging me out of bed, I doubt that William Petrie or the captain will be looking at my shirt.'

He sat down on the side of the bed, put on socks and shoes and quickly laced them up. 'I'll try not to be too long,' he said, as he headed for the door.

It closed behind him, and Jane lay back on the pillow with another sigh. She feared that their peaceful holiday was about to become anything but.

CHAPTER 6

'Who found the body?'

'The steward allocated to Pashley's cabin,' said Petrie. 'He knocked on the door at six o'clock. Apparently, no matter how late Pashley went to bed, he always wanted to be woken early. The steward couldn't get an answer, so he used his pass key to look in to make sure Pashley was alright. The fellow said Pashley was so regular in his habits that he was concerned for him.'

De Silva studied the inert form sprawled on the bed. Pashley's dinner jacket was unbuttoned and his bow tie askew, but his immaculate white dress shirt was unsullied. His sightless, bloodshot eyes were burning pools in an otherwise grey face. His mouth gaped, forced open by the soggy, bilious-yellow mass of newspaper that had been rammed into it. There was a smell of whisky, ink, and vomit.

'The ship's doctor is on his way,' said the captain in a strong Scottish accent.

'Do you have any idea how many people know about this, sir?' asked de Silva.

'The steward who found him, obviously, and the officer I sent to fetch you. I wouldn't have involved him, but the steward was in too agitated a state to be trusted with a message. Otherwise only us three and Brady, the ship's doctor.'

The captain flashed de Silva a grim look. 'And it's to stay that way, do you understand? I won't have this getting out and causing panic on my ship. Everything will proceed normally. Even when this villain has been apprehended, it's much better for the passengers, and the crew, to remain in blissful ignorance.'

De Silva weighed up the situation and decided not to argue, at least for the time being. There were bound to be people he needed to question, but the murderer had to be on the ship, so until they reached Port Said, his or her only escape would be into the sea: not an enticing option for most people. Returning to port at Bombay might well make it easier for them to evade capture. He nodded. 'I understand, sir.'

'How long will it take you to find the culprit?'

The sharpness with which the captain delivered the question took de Silva aback. Then he realised that, despite his seniority, the man was rattled. Many of his passengers were wealthy and distinguished. A serious crime on board would reflect badly on the reputation of the ship. He wanted to put the matter behind him as soon as possible.

'It's hard to say, sir.'

The captain's brow furrowed. He grunted, but de Silva resolved to keep his own irritation to himself. It would do no good to fall out with the man.

'Very early days to answer that question, McDowell,' interjected William Petrie. 'But I have tremendous faith in Inspector de Silva. As I told you, we're lucky to have him on board.'

McDowell's voice took on a more emollient tone. 'Do your best, Inspector. If anyone asks, I'll have it put about that Pashley died of natural causes. A heart attack: that shouldn't cause alarm.'

There was a knock at the door and Doctor Brady came in. He was an elderly man, short and rotund with thinning grey hair. 'I see you don't need me to tell you that the gentleman's dead,' he observed wryly. He spoke with an Irish brogue. 'At what time was he found?'

'Six o'clock,' said Captain McDowell. 'He was found by the night steward who was due to go off duty an hour later.'

'A strange time to enter a passenger's cabin, to be sure. What was the reason for such an early call? Was the deceased merely keen, like Orpheus, to greet the dawn?'

'I understand from the steward that Pashley filed daily articles for the society column of *The Monocle*,' put in William Petrie. 'It's a London paper he wrote for. He composed the articles during the day then later liked to spend half an hour or so polishing his work. The steward collected each dispatch in the early morning and took it the radio room. From there, it was radioed to London, arriving ready for publication in the next edition. I believe a tip usually changed hands, perhaps explaining the steward's conscientiousness.'

'Who was the last person to see him alive?' asked de Silva.

'Apart from the murderer? Probably the steward. He saw Pashley go to his cabin at around one o'clock in the morning.'

That was interesting, thought de Silva. The occupants of the noisy table where Pashley had been sitting at dinner had been conspicuous on the dance floor, but now he came to think of it, he hadn't noticed Pashley among them after the meal had ended.

'He may have gone to the bar,' said William Petrie when he mentioned it. 'That's easily checked. The steward mentioned something about Pashley seeming to have had a lot to drink. He'd lost his key and the steward had to let him into his cabin.'

Doctor Brady approached the bed and examined the corpse.

'Rigor mortis is minimal,' he murmured. He straightened up. 'I estimate that the time of death was around four o'clock this morning.'

Gently, he pulled at the newspaper jutting from Pashley's mouth. 'This was pretty firmly jammed into the windpipe.' He tugged a little harder and a wedge of paper came out. He laid it on the bed then bent down and peered more closely at Pashley's face. 'The nostrils have been sealed off too. A classic case of asphyxiation, albeit by somewhat unorthodox means. But as there's no sign of a struggle, I deduce that Pashley was sedated before the attack.'

'Can you tell us more?' asked Petrie.

Brady shrugged. 'From the smell, he drank a good deal of whisky not long before he died, but I can't say for sure whether it would have been enough to make him dead drunk. It's possible his drink was spiked as well.'

'With what?'

'There are several possibilities, but I suspect the most likely is chloral hydrate. It takes between twenty and sixty minutes to incapacitate a man, so that would give time for him to return to his cabin. Some people say the substance gives off the smell of oranges, but I've never noticed it myself.'

De Silva recalled a book of true crimes he had once read on Jane's recommendation. In one that had occurred about twenty years previously, several bar owners and over a hundred waiters had been arrested in the city of Chicago in America. They were convicted of spiking the drinks of customers who didn't tip generously enough, then robbing them. The spiked drink used was named after the bar owner who had invented the trick, but de Silva couldn't recall his name.

'Would there be any other signs that it's been ingested?' he asked Brady.

'Prior to loss of consciousness? Slurred speech; difficulty walking—'

'But then a casual observer might simply assume Pashley was drunk,' said Petrie.

'Indeed.'

'Can this chloral hydrate be detected in the body?'

'No. That's why I believe it may have been the method the killer chose.'

Captain McDowell donned the cap he had removed out of respect for the dead man. 'I must return to the bridge before my absence causes comment. My apologies for leaving you with this problem, Petrie.' He delved in his pocket and handed over two keys. 'The steward's pass key and a spare. You may need them.'

De Silva wondered whether he imagined that Petrie threw a wry glance at the captain's retreating figure. Doubtless he didn't relish the prospect of this interruption to his holiday. The door closed, and Petrie turned to Doctor Brady. 'May I rely on you to make arrangements to remove the body to a more suitable place until we decide how best to bury it?'

'Certainly.'

'As Captain McDowell says, the matter needs handling very discreetly to avoid alarming the passengers. If there's suitable space available, he may prefer to hold the body in cold storage until it can be quietly handed over to the authorities at Port Said for them to deal with. Otherwise, Pashley will have to be buried as sea which may invite more attention. I recall from my naval days that there are formalities to be observed, including stopping the ship while the burial takes place.'

'Leave it to me.'

'Good man. Here, take one of these keys so you can come and go as you need.'

'Thank you.'

When Brady had gone, William Petrie flopped down in the armchair by the bed. His coolness in proximity to the dead man made de Silva wonder how often he had faced death in his life.

'Once again, my apologies for involving you, de Silva, but I'm going to need help with this one.'

'That's quite alright, sir. I'm happy to do anything I can to assist.'

'Excellent. Well, where do you recommend that we start?'

'I'd like to make a thorough search of the body and the cabin before we do anything else. After that, the steward needs to be questioned again.'

'And the bar steward on duty that evening in the Cabin Class bar, if Pashley was there,' Petrie said. 'He mustn't be told the whole story, of course. We'll only tell him that we need to piece together the events leading to Pashley's heart attack.'

Pausing, he threw de Silva a sideways glance. 'McDowell's a good man at heart. I've known him many years. We served together in the Navy in the Great War. He chose to make the seafaring life his career afterwards, while I opted for the Colonial Service. My family have a long history of service in it.'

He took a gold cigarette case out of his pocket. 'D'you smoke?'

'No, thank you, sir.'

Petrie lit up. 'I find it helps the concentration. Tell me, did you believe the good doctor when he said there's no method for detecting chloral hydrate?'

'I wasn't absolutely convinced. To my mind, he was rather too quick to dismiss the idea. I've had many conversations with one of the senior medical men at Kandy, a Doctor Van Bruyn.'

'Henry Van Bruyn? I think I know him. Highly respected in his field.'

'Yes. I understand from him that great strides are being made in the detection of many drugs.'

'In other words, a less trenchant denial would have inspired more confidence in you.'

'It would, but I may be wrong.'

'I believe Brady has qualifications from the best medical schools in Dublin, but I imagine he obtained those many years ago. Nowadays, he may be behind the times. In any case, we're on a ship, not in a laboratory. In this heat, if there's no suitable place to keep it, the body will have to be disposed of before we reach Port Said. Do you think your investigation will be compromised?'

De Silva shook his head. 'Not especially. It's very likely something was administered, but it may not be relevant to know exactly what it was.' The name of the criminal bartender in Chicago came back to him: Mickey Finn.

Petrie reached for an ashtray and stubbed out his half-smoked cigarette. 'Only time will tell, and time's something we don't have a great deal of. We'd better get on with searching the body.'

The pockets of Pashley's jacket and trousers revealed only a few items, and they were what might be expected – a cigarette case, a gold lighter, a wallet, a handful of loose change, and a spotless linen handkerchief.

When they had finished, Petrie folded Pashley's hands on his chest and pulled up the sheet to cover his face. 'The poor chap is entitled to some respect,' he said. 'I'm afraid it's unlikely he'll be buried on home soil.'

They started to go through the cabin. Clearly, the dead man hadn't stinted on his clothing. The cupboards contained numerous elegant suits; some of them cut from cream or fawn linen. Others were made of herringbone tweed. There were also a dove-grey barathea overlaid with a fine red stripe, a Lovat green wool, and a navy Prince of Wales check. There were cream Oxford bags, dress shirts and soft shirts in white or pastel colours, cashmere jumpers, formal ties and paisley cravats, leather gloves, silk socks and underwear, and several hats. On the lowest shelf, two-tone and plain black or navy leather brogues were precisely aligned in rows.

'Lock & Co,' said Petrie, picking up a Homburg hat and turning it round to read the label. 'And all the other items are good makes. Writing treated Mr Pashley kindly. Unless he had family money to call on as well.'

In the small bathroom, a shaving kit from Trumpers of Curzon Street, a bottle of cologne, and a few other expensive-looking toiletries yielded no clues. De Silva returned to the bedroom to find Petrie looking at the books on the bedside table. 'Hardly what one would call a literary selection — a few lurid thrillers. From the way Pashley dressed, I'm surprised his taste in books wasn't more highbrow. His writing materials are in the drawers below, along with his passport, his ticket, and various notes and other papers, but no sign of an article for the radio office to send out this morning. He must have been too incapacitated to work.'

De Silva frowned. 'But didn't the steward say he usually started to write his articles during the day?'

'What do you mean?'

'It seems odd we've found nothing for a current one, even if only a rough draft.'

Petrie shrugged. 'Presumably he didn't write anything during the day this time. He probably would have last night if he hadn't been knocked out by whatever he drank. Anything else you want to look at?'

'I'd like to stay for a while, sir. Sometimes it helps to get a feel for a place.'

'Very well. I'll call in on my wife and reassure her. She'll be anxious to know why I was summoned so early this morning.'

'What will you tell her?'

'I believe I can trust her with the truth. Lady Caroline is very discreet when she needs to be.' He smiled. 'I imagine it will be hard to keep it from Mrs de Silva.'

'It will.'

'Then we may have two lady sleuths to assist us in our

endeavours.' He handed de Silva the second key. 'I doubt I need remind you to lock up when you go. I suggest you return it to the duty steward when you've finished. Pashley's key is still missing.'

He threw a glance of distaste at the wedge of newspaper Doctor Brady had removed from the dead man's mouth. 'I suppose that needs investigation,' he added.

The unpleasant thought had occurred to de Silva too that someone ought to do their best to examine as much as possible of the newspaper; it might contain an article or articles that would provide a clue to the identity of the murderer. His nose wrinkled at the prospect, but he nodded. 'I'll see to it, sir.'

The door closed behind Petrie; de Silva looked about him. He wasn't entirely sure what he was looking for, but he always liked to have a few quiet moments at the scene of a crime. There had been occasions when it had proved useful.

He'd start with the furnishings. The cabin was supplied with similar items to those in Tourist Class, but they were more luxurious. The bed where Pashley lay was covered by a satin eiderdown.

The possibilities there exhausted, de Silva turned with reluctance to the newspaper, teasing apart the wedge Doctor Brady had removed from Pashley's mouth. He wasn't worried about destroying evidence. Even if he'd had his fingerprinting equipment with him, he very much doubted there would be any to find on the soggy paper. The sheets of paper were from *The Colombo Times*. He noted the date. It was the day they had left Colombo. Unfortunately, that didn't narrow the field much. It merely showed Pashley's killer had joined the ship in Colombo, or already been on it, that's if indeed the paper belonged to the killer. The articles that remained legible gave no indication they were relevant. In any case, none of them had been written by Pashley.

He went to the small bathroom and washed and dried

his hands. When he returned, he once more checked over the carpet and behind the curtains as well as closely inspecting the dark-blue velvet that covered the armchairs. No tears or holes where anything might be concealed. It occurred to him that they had forgotten to check the top of the wardrobe. As he reached up, his eye fell on a strand of grey wool that had adhered to the sleeve of his jacket. He picked it off and studied it. It didn't look to be from any of the grey suits or jumpers in the wardrobe. The strand was thicker and of rougher texture. He looked around for more but found none. Possibly the strand had caught on his sleeve when he checked the curtains or the floor. It was probably unimportant, but out of force of habit, he put it in his pocket.

All he found on the top of the wardrobe was a thin layer of dust. He brushed it off his hands and sat down in one of the armchairs for a while, his eyes drawn to the body on the bed.

Petrie was right. Pashley's taste in reading was odd for a man whose taste in other possessions seemed so refined. He needed to find out more about this man, and time was limited. When the ship reached Port Said, unless all the passengers were put under arrest, it would be impossible to prevent any of them leaving the ship.

He was also supposed to be on holiday. Just as well, he thought ruefully, that the pyramids weren't going anywhere in a hurry.

CHAPTER 7

De Silva interviewed the steward in a cramped room on one of the lower decks. Part of the crew's quarters, it was stuffy, and the air reverberated constantly with the thrum of the ship's propellers.

The steward, a Hong Kong Chinese called Chung, regarded de Silva with frightened eyes. Sweat marked the underarms of his tunic and his forehead glistened. Even allowing for the heat in the small room, de Silva believed it evidenced genuine terror. He was inclined to accept the man's protestations that he was innocent. In de Silva's experience, villains were usually more composed at the initial stage of questioning. They had honed their responses and were careful not to show alarm. It was only if one was able to catch them out later that the protective shell crumbled.

'What time do you come on duty?' asked de Silva.

'At seven o'clock in the evening, sir. I work through the night and go to my bunk at seven the next morning. I sleep for a few hours then have duties as a kitchen porter in the middle of the day.' Chung licked his dry lips. He pushed a lock of black hair out of his eyes. De Silva saw that his hand trembled.

'Do you need some water?'

A look of gratitude came over the steward's face. 'Thank you, sir.'

There was a small metal basin in one corner of the room.

De Silva went to it and filled the tumbler on the back of the surround. He gave it to Chung. The steward gulped down the contents then wiped his mouth with the back of his hand.

'So,' de Silva continued, 'I presume you see the passengers in your section when they go to dinner?'

'Yes, sir, and when they come back later when they are ready to sleep.'

'At what time did Mr Pashley return to his cabin?'

'It was just after one o'clock.'

'And how did he seem to you?'

'I think he'd had plenty to drink,' said Chung cautiously. 'He said he had lost his key and needed me to let him into his cabin.'

So far so good, thought de Silva. The man wasn't diverging from the story he had told Petrie and Captain McDowell. It was always worthwhile checking the facts in case there was some interesting inconsistency. He had seen the place where the steward sat in this section of the ship, on duty in case any of the Cabin Class passengers required something at any time of the day or night. It was no bigger than a cupboard in the corridor lobby. From it, he had a view down the corridor, and would see anyone leaving or entering the corridor, or their cabin.

'Was Mr Pashley the last to retire for the night?'

'No, sir. Mrs March and Mr Chiltern came back at about two o'clock, but the rest were all in their cabins before midnight and didn't leave them again until the morning.'

'Did Mrs March or Mr Chiltern leave their cabins again? Or did anyone else come or go? A maid or a valet, perhaps?'

For a beat, de Silva sensed that Chung hesitated, but the moment soon passed. 'Mrs March has a maid who stays to help her get ready for bed, and Mr Chiltern has a valet. They both passed me going back to their quarters in Third

Class at about half past two, otherwise no one; the maids for Mrs Pilkington and Mrs de Vere were gone long before.'

'What about the other passengers' staff?'

'They have none, sir. They use the crew's service for anything they need.'

'Did you hear any noises later? People walking about? Doors opening or closing?'

'Nothing like that. Everything was quiet.'

'And you didn't leave your post until you went to call Mr Pashley?'

Chung cast a hopeful glance at the empty tumbler on the table, but de Silva decided he could wait this time.

'I repeat: did you leave your post?'

'No, sir,' said Chung unhappily.

'You're certain?'

'Yes.'

* * *

It was a relief to escape the stuffy crew quarters and sit in the Petries' spacious stateroom. The blades of a large brass and mahogany ceiling fan swished, cooling the air. Framed by a wide window, the Arabian Sea glittered in the sunshine.

'Anything to report from your interview with the steward?' asked William Petrie. They were alone. Once Lady Caroline had learnt what had happened, she'd offered to visit Jane and enlighten her.

De Silva went briefly through the gist of the interview.

'Hmm, nothing new there then. What impression did you have of the fellow?'

'I thought he was probably trustworthy; although he did hesitate when I asked if anyone had come past him after the passengers on that corridor had retired for the night.'

'Do you think he was lying about that?'

'Hard to say.' De Silva shrugged. 'I suppose he might have nodded off. It's a long night, and he works a shift as a kitchen porter in the day too.'

Petrie nodded. 'The heat in those kitchens must be intense. Exhausting for any man, even if he's used to it.'

'All the same, his post isn't exactly luxurious. I imagine it would be difficult to do more than doze fitfully on the hard chair he's provided with.'

A pack of playing cards lay on the table between them, alongside a hefty tome entitled *The Life of Gladstone*, a few fashion magazines, and a sunhat made of superfine straw. William Petrie picked up the cards and shuffled them. De Silva wondered whether it was his way of helping himself to concentrate on a problem.

Petrie spoke: 'Three staterooms and four inside cabins lead off the corridor where Pashley was lodged. We're only concerned with the corridor on the port side of the ship. Access to the corridor on the starboard side, which has the same number and layout of staterooms and cabins, is through a separate door. In both cases, there are always stewards on duty just inside the doors.'

He dealt the king and queen of diamonds. 'I have the names of the other passengers on the corridor now. Arthur Chiltern and his fiancée Diana March occupy the first and second staterooms, followed by Mrs Pilkington. She has the largest one, in the bow.' He placed the queen of spades next to the other two cards. 'The black widow, as she's known in a card game my wife is fond of.'

De Silva remembered the three people from dinner the previous evening.

Next, Petrie put down the queen of hearts. 'A Mrs de Vere occupies the largest of the inside cabins across the corridor. Lady Caroline informs me that the lady writes very popular romantic novels in a sentimental vein. In the remaining inside cabins, we have a clergyman, Canon George Ryder.' He put down the jack of spades. 'I don't know much about him. I'll ask Captain McDowell if he can give me some information. I must say, it rather surprises me that he travels Cabin Class. A canon ranks above a parish priest, but I doubt he'd be able to afford the fare on a stipend alone.'

He scratched his chin. 'Inherited money's a possibility, I suppose. Then there's a woman called Meadows, who has the unenviable job of being companion and general factotum to Mrs Pilkington.' He added the ace of clubs. 'I assume Mrs Pilkington pays Cabin Class for her so that the unfortunate woman can be at her beck and call at a moment's notice. And lastly, Charles Pashley, the joker in the pack.' He placed the joker card next to the others.

De Silva studied the cards with their stylised pictures and sharply contrasting reds, blacks and golds. All these passengers would need to be interviewed. Hoping Petrie agreed, he waited to hear what he was going to say about that.

Petrie scooped up the cards. 'I'm afraid the Pilkington woman is liable to be difficult, but Ryder seems a mild kind of chap from what little I've seen of him. If Mrs Meadows is as much under Clara Pilkington's thumb as I believe her to be, we might not get much out of her, but that may well be unimportant. Diana March is a charming woman from what I've seen. I expect she'll be cooperative, and unless Archie Chiltern's time in Hong Kong has radically changed him, he's likely to be obliging too. As for Mrs de Vere, I hope it won't be hard to win her cooperation, although I'll be surprised if she has anything useful to impart.'

De Silva wondered why Petrie made that assumption. Was it simply because he had no time for romantic novelists?

'Well, de Silva,' William Petrie went on. 'I don't know about you, but I'm famished. I think we should allow ourselves a late breakfast before we begin. I'm afraid it may cause comment if you join me. Shall we meet back here in two hours? After I've eaten, I'll speak with Captain McDowell. He won't be happy about our questioning passengers, and I see his point of view, but it must be done. I'm confident I'll persuade him in the end, even if his word is law on this ship.'

'What about their staff, sir? Maids, valets – I understand that some of the Cabin Class passengers have them.'

'A good thought. I'll deal with that when I speak to him. Oh, and you'd better find out who was on duty at the bar that evening. It will be hard to keep it under your hat why you're asking about Pashley, so don't forget the heart attack story.'

'Very well, sir.'

'Good man. I'll see you in two hours. I'll give instructions to the staff at the entrance to Cabin Class that you're to come and go as you please.'

CHAPTER 8

De Silva ate a speedy meal of eggs and fruit in the restaurant. The place was almost deserted. By now, most people would have eaten breakfast and gone off to stroll on deck or relax in the sunshine. Torn between missing Jane and an undeniable feeling of excitement, he considered the challenge facing him. He was sorry it had arisen because of another's misfortune, but the prospect of pitting his wits against criminal minds always set his blood racing.

He popped a sugar lump into his second cup of tea, staring down into the fragrant amber brew as the granules dissolved. It was mid-morning, so the bar staff in Cabin Class should be on duty ready to serve pre-lunch customers. One thing he had noticed about being on a cruise ship was that there were very few times when passengers were not eating or drinking.

At the entrance to Cabin Class, he gave his name and was waved through. He soon found the bar, a magnificent room where tables and chairs were disposed around the central, circular counter like moons orbiting a planet. The front of the counter was upholstered in cream and black leather and its top was of black marble. Tall, crystal-glass sculptures in the shape of fountains displayed champagne glasses. On the wall behind the counter, shelves were stocked with a huge variety of spirits, aperitifs and liqueurs. De Silva's sensitive nose picked out the aromas of whisky, rum, and gin mingled with the scents of mint, orange, cherry, and herbs.

A lone bar steward was polishing a cocktail glass with a soft cloth. He quickly put it down when he saw de Silva.

'Good morning, sir. What can I get you?'

'Thank you, but it's a little early for me. I've come for some information. Sadly, one of the passengers was taken seriously ill last night. I'm trying to piece together what he was doing in the hours before he collapsed.'

A look of alarm entered the bar steward's eyes.

'Don't worry,' de Silva added hastily. 'No one is accusing you or your colleagues of wrongdoing. We simply want to find out as much as possible about the passenger's movements. Were you on duty yesterday evening?'

The man nodded. 'Myself and two others, sir.'

'Are they here?'

'Yes.'

'Then fetch them, please.'

The man disappeared for a few moments then came back with his colleagues. They shook their heads when de Silva described Pashley. 'I don't think the gentleman drank here last night, sir,' said the first steward. 'But I can tell you for sure if you'll wait a moment.'

He went to a drawer and, producing a large book, opened it and ran his finger down the columns ruled on the page. 'There's no entry for Mr Pashley, sir. We have to keep a daily record of all drinks purchased so that the accounts for the passengers' bar bills can be made up at the end of the voyage.'

De Silva peered at the page upside down. 'Let me see.'

The steward swivelled the book and de Silva inspected the names. The fellow was right. Pashley's name wasn't there. He supposed it was possible that someone else had bought his drinks, but the bar staff seemed very sure they hadn't seen him that evening.

'Alright, thank you.'

So, wondered de Silva as he left the bar, where had Pashley been between finishing dinner and returning to his cabin at one o'clock? From what de Silva had observed, Pashley hadn't been drinking excessively at dinner, even if the rest of his party had. Had he spent the time after dinner drinking more? If not at the Cabin Class bar, then he might have been in someone's cabin, and it would be very interesting to know whose. The other possibility was that he had gone to the bar in Tourist Class. A pity it was the night he and Jane had been invited by the Petries, or they might have spotted him there.

On his way out of the bar, de Silva met William Petrie coming the other way.

'Any luck?' asked Petrie.

'I'm afraid not, sir. The bar stewards were on duty last night and seem very sure our man wasn't drinking there after dinner. In fact, they showed me the account ledger to prove it. I was just going to the bar in Tourist Class to check if he went there.'

'I'll join you.'

The bar in Tourist Class was a considerably more modest affair than the splendid one in Cabin Class. It yielded more satisfactory information, however. One of the younger bar stewards remembered serving Charles Pashley.

'Was he drinking with any of the other passengers?'

'It's very busy here in the evenings, sir. I can't be sure.'

'I saw him talking to one of the crew,' another steward chimed in.

Picking up gossip, no doubt, thought de Silva.

'Had he come here before?'

'Quite a few times, sir.'

'Where's the ledger for drinks purchased? I'd like to see it.'

The young man looked uncertainly at one of his more senior colleagues, who nodded.

Petrie and de Silva studied the entries. It was clear that Pashley had drunk at this bar several times, including on the eve of his last night on earth. But who had he been with? He had only ordered one double whisky. Surely that wouldn't be enough to tip him over into the inebriated state in which the steward claimed he arrived back to his cabin? Was someone else buying? Or was Doctor Brady right, and there was more in Pashley's whisky glass than alcohol?

Looking round the bar, de Silva tried to imagine the room when it was full. There were plenty of booths and dark corners. Easy for two people to get lost in the crowd.

'That leaves us no further forward,' remarked William Petrie as they returned to the lobby outside the bar. 'Still, early days. Why don't you go and have a word with your wife, de Silva? Let her know you're alright. Then we can convene in my cabin and decide where to go next with our inquiries.'

* * *

'Poor Mr Pashley. It sounds as if he suffered a particularly unpleasant death,' said Jane when de Silva had filled her in on the details. Lady Caroline had told her no more than Charles Pashley had been found murdered in his cabin.

'William Petrie's going to speak to the captain. He thinks there'll be some resistance to our questioning the other passengers whose cabins are on the same corridor.'

'Why does he think that?'

'The captain's very anxious not to spread rumours and panic on the ship.'

'It would be unfortunate, I agree, but what's the alternative?'

'Sweeping the whole thing under the carpet, and that may result in the murderer getting away with his crime.'

'Even the captain can't believe that would be justified,' said Jane frowning.

'I hope not. Anyway, I'm sure William Petrie can be persuasive when he wants to be.'

'You said everything was left tidy in Pashley's cabin, so it seems unlikely the motive was theft, although I suppose there could be something small, like a piece of jewellery the thief was after. But then why the elaborate business with the newspaper? Wouldn't a burglar simply knock Pashley out and get away with whatever he wanted as quickly as possible?'

'One would think so.'

'What about revenge? I gather from Lady Caroline that he upset a lot of people over the course of his career. Perhaps that's the significance of the newspaper.'

'Or the murderer wants us to think that.'

They both pondered the problem.

'Who hated Charles Pashley enough to murder him?' mused Jane. 'Might the editor of the paper he wrote for be able to help us? Aggrieved people often write letters to editors complaining about derogatory articles.'

De Silva smiled ruefully. 'It's not a bad idea, my love, but I'm sure it would be the last thing the captain would agree to. If he doesn't want it known on the ship that there's been a murder, he certainly won't want it broadcast all over London. He's bound to refuse to send a message to the editor unless he's absolutely sure he can trust him, and a story like this might be too tempting not to print.'

'I suppose you're right. So, what are you going to do next?'

'Find William Petrie and decide how to go about interviewing the other passengers whose accommodation is on the same corridor as Pashley's. Of course, we can't be sure yet that the steward's telling the truth that no one apart from the six of them and Pashley went past him after dinner, but even if he's not, they're all still under suspicion. I must admit, I'm not looking forward to the task. I'll be glad to have William Petrie along to back me up.'

CHAPTER 9

Before de Silva had the chance to go up to the Petries' state-room, a message came from William that he would meet him on the Promenade Deck. Looking for him, de Silva passed a few uniformed maids out exercising their Cabin Class employers' lap dogs, and other passengers reclining on sun loungers in the shade, dozing or reading. Stewards hovered in case their services were required.

Otherwise, the deck was deserted. Its polished teak boards gleamed. Every painted surface was a brilliant white; brass fittings winked in the sunshine. The strong smell of salt on the breeze made de Silva think of the fish market in Colombo. When he was a boy and left occasionally in the care of the family's cook, he had been taken there sometimes. He remembered the mass of stalls piled with glistening, scaly produce: parrotfish, grouper, barracuda, and giant prawns. There had also been lobsters – fascinat-ingly sinister to a small boy – and great hunks of shark, tuna and swordfish.

'Ah, there you are, de Silva. Sorry to change the plan. Lady Caroline's resting, and I don't want to disturb her.' William Petrie strode towards him, smiling. 'I thought it would be quiet here, and a turn around the deck might help to clear our heads, eh? Shall we walk?'

'Certainly.'

'I've squared things with Captain McDowell. He was

reluctant, but he accepts we need to question the other passengers on Pashley's corridor. He was less willing where maids and valets are concerned, and I can't budge him. He's convinced that will lead to rumours going around the ship.'

It seemed unfair to de Silva that Captain McDowell assumed maids and valets would be looser tongued than their employers. Clearly, he didn't believe in democracy on his ship.

'I'll leave it for now,' Petrie went on, 'but I've already sent a message to Clara Pilkington asking if we may visit her. We're invited for tea. Now, I'll tell you what I already know about her.'

De Silva waited expectantly.

'Her husband made a fortune in coal mining in the north of England,' Petrie continued. 'Neither of them was born into high society. He was none the worse for that, but as you may have noticed, her lack of good breeding can have unfortunate results. Pilkington's been dead for years – it must be at least ten now. Since then, she's thrown her considerable energies and funds into the social whirl. She entertains the great and the good when they'll accept her invitations and denigrates them when they won't.'

De Silva nodded. 'What do you think is the best way to approach her, sir?'

'If possible, I'd still rather we kept it quiet that we have a case of murder on our hands. We stick to the story that Pashley died of natural causes, and we're merely following the usual procedure where there are no witnesses to a sudden death. Someone will have to report to the coroner at Port Said, and so on. I'll say I've offered to relieve the captain of the job of collecting statements for that purpose, and in view of your professional experience, I've asked you to assist me. After that, I'll ask a few questions about what she was doing that night and how well she knew Pashley. If you agree, I'll do the talking and leave you to observe her reactions.'

'Very well.'

De Silva didn't like to criticise Petrie's plan, but he was doubtful that the matter was going to be quite so straightforward. He had the impression that Mrs Pilkington was too wily to swallow the story of a natural death. She also seemed to be one of those ladies, fired in the kilns of England's green and pleasant land, who had then been thickly glazed with an unshakeable sense of their own rightness and superiority. She was unlikely to be over-encumbered with patience or the inclination to be cooperative if she wasn't let in on the truth. Their only hope was that her desire to ingratiate herself with Petrie, as an entrée into Lady Caroline's society, was sufficiently strong for him to be able to conduct the conversation on his own terms.

Petrie looked at his watch. 'She's expecting us in her stateroom at four o'clock. It's after three now.' He gestured to a pair of steamer chairs in the shade. 'Shall we sit down? I'm in need of a smoke.'

Long legs stretched out in the steamer chair, he pulled a packet of cigarettes from the pocket of his linen jacket and offered one to de Silva. 'Change your mind?'

'No, thank you, sir.'

Petrie lit up and inhaled deeply, then blew out a ring of smoke. 'Does your wife have an opinion on this business? I understand from Archie Clutterbuck that she has a good instinct for this kind of thing, and we're going to need all the help we can get with this one.'

'We agreed it's far too early to come to any conclusions, but she thought it was unlikely that the motive was theft.'

'I agree with her.' He signalled to a steward who brought an ashtray. 'So what else? Blackmail? Revenge? A spurned lover? Whatever it was, we need to work quickly. Once we reach Port Said, it will be difficult to prevent people leaving the ship.'

They sat in silence, contemplating the sea. With a flutter

of feathers, a seagull landed on the rail nearby. It folded its black-tipped wings and tilted its head, regarding them with a malevolent eye.

'Never liked those birds,' observed Petrie. 'Scavengers. And I never thought I'd want to go near the sea again. The ship McDowell and I served on went down at Jutland. We were lucky to survive. Many good men didn't.'

'I'm sorry, sir,' said de Silva, not knowing what else to say.

Petrie sighed. 'Life goes on.'

He glanced again at his watch. 'Speaking of which, I think it's time we were off to see Mrs Pilkington.'

* * *

The drawing room of Clara Pilkington's stateroom in the bow was extremely elegant with a magnificent, uninterrupted view of the sea. Primrose-yellow walls set off ebony-inlaid, rosewood furniture in the French style, and there were antique armchairs and a chaise longue in a deeper shade of yellow. A large mirror, shaped like a sunburst, reflected a tall bronze vase filled with lilies. Their heavy fragrance competed for supremacy with the scent drifting from another arrangement of flowers in the Chinese bowl on the low coffee table. Beside it was a crisply folded copy of *The Times of India*. Presumably it had been brought on board at Bombay.

Mrs Pilkington wore a pale-blue, flowery tea gown in which no opportunity for ruffles had been overlooked. Her jewellery was more restrained than it had been the previous evening, but her fingers were still loaded with rings. She merely gave de Silva a peremptory nod but extended a hand for William Petrie to kiss.

'Do sit down.'

'Thank you, it's very good of you to see Inspector de Silva and I at such short notice.'

Clara Pilkington shot an impatient glance towards a corner of the room. For the first time, de Silva noticed that a severe-looking woman stood there. She was plainly dressed, with iron-grey hair. He guessed she was in her mid to late forties.

'Have you ordered the tea?' Clara Pilkington asked her snappishly.

'Yes, I'm sure they won't be much longer.'

With a grudging nod, Clara Pilkington turned back to William Petrie. 'My companion and secretary, Mrs Angela Meadows.'

There was a knock at the door, and Mrs Meadows hurried to open it. A steward pushed in a trolley laden with all the accoutrements of an English afternoon tea. De Silva felt a little more cheerful.

The business of filling cups and arranging plates of sandwiches, scones and cakes took a few minutes then the steward withdrew.

'Do help yourself, Mr Petrie,' said Clara Pilkington. 'Oh, and you too, Inspector de Silva.'

'Thank you, ma'am.'

It was the first time she had acknowledged his presence, but de Silva consoled himself with the thought that the scones and cream cakes looked excellent. He did as he had been invited.

'Now, my dear Mr Petrie,' she went on. 'I'm quite sure that as you've taken the trouble to come to see me, there's more to that man Pashley's demise than natural causes.'

Ah, Clara Pilkington might be disagreeable, but as he had suspected, she was no fool. So much for the story of a heart attack.

'You are a step ahead of me already, Mrs Pilkington,' said Petrie. If he was disconcerted, he had too much self-control to show it.

Clara gave him a satisfied smile. 'My husband used to

say that most people would need to get up extremely early in the morning if they wished to be ahead of *me*.'

'I hope you won't be offended if I stress that it's of the utmost importance that no talk of murder gets around the ship.'

'Not at all, my dear sir.' She waved a dismissive hand at her companion. 'And you needn't trouble yourself about Meadows. But I'm afraid I can't be of any help to you. Of course, I knew Charley Pashley slightly. Most people in London society did, but I had very little to do with him. A tiresome man with those waspish articles of his. I presume he thought they passed for wit.'

'Just for the record, may I ask what your movements were last night?'

'Certainly. As you may recall, I dined at the captain's table. Afterwards, we listened to the orchestra for a while. They played Strauss – delightful. My maid and Meadows helped me get ready for bed just before midnight. I don't sleep well, so Meadows prepared my usual powder. After that, I was dead to the world until morning.'

An unfortunate choice of phrase thought de Silva.

'What about you, Mrs Meadows?'

'My meal was brought to me in my cabin. It's one of the ones along this corridor on the opposite side, next to Canon Ryder's.'

'Meadows prefers to dine quietly,' Clara Pilkington interposed.

De Silva wondered if Mrs Meadows was ever given the option of expressing her own wishes, although from her demeanour, she looked as if she would not be too easily put upon.

A fleshy petal slipped from one of the lilies in the bronze vase and fell onto the onyx top of the pedestal on which the vase stood, taking with it a light dusting of orange pollen from the flower's stamens. Mrs Pilkington tutted. 'I hate it when flowers are not fresh. Why haven't you seen to these already, Meadows? Get them changed.'

'Yes, Mrs Pilkington.'

'Did you hear any unusual noises once you were back in your cabin?' William Petrie asked quickly, covering the awkward moment.

'No. As I said, I prepared for bed, then took the sleeping draught.'

'What about you, Mrs Meadows?'

'None.'

'Can either of you ladies tell me anything about the occupants of the other cabins?'

Clara Pilkington dabbed a trace of thick cream from her upper lip with a lace-edged handkerchief. 'Mrs March and her *innamorato*, Arthur Chiltern, are very slight acquaintances.' Her expression suggested that she didn't wish them to become anything more. 'Naturally, I know the Chilterns in London. Meadows can tell you more about Venetia de Vere than I can. You're fond of her sentimental outpourings, aren't you, Meadows?'

'I admit I do have a weakness for romantic fiction, but I wouldn't describe myself as a confidante of Mrs de Vere.'

With amusement, de Silva noticed a spark of mutiny in the companion's eyes.

'Pour me another cup of tea,' Clara Pilkington said tetchily. 'And don't neglect our guests. Sometimes I wonder what I pay you for.'

'The other resident on this corridor is Canon George Ryder. Are you acquainted with him?' asked Petrie.

Clara Pilkington waved a hand at her secretary. 'Merely a nodding acquaintance. Meadows can tell you about him. She attends chapel regularly.'

'I believe Canon Ryder retired recently from his post at the Anglican cathedral of St John in Hong Kong,' said Mrs Meadows. 'He does attend chapel – not in an official capacity you understand, as the ship has a chaplain. I'm sorry, I can't tell you more. Canon Ryder seems a very private man.'

* * *

'I'm afraid that wasn't very illuminating,' said Petrie when they had thanked their hostess and left her. He set a brisk pace along the deck. The sky was still the intense blue of the cornflowers de Silva grew in the garden at Sunnybank for Jane. He felt a trickle of sweat on his cheek.

Petrie lit another cigarette and smoked for a while in silence. 'Tell me what you thought, de Silva,' he said at last.

'I'm inclined to believe Mrs Pilkington, sir. If I'm wrong, she's an accomplished liar.'

Petrie chuckled. 'To add to all her other good qualities, eh?'

De Silva smiled.

'What about the Meadows woman? She must have the patience of Job. Imagine a life spent in the service of Mrs Pilkington. No, I'm sure you'd rather not.'

There was another pause.

'Somehow, I doubt she's implicated, but I'll make discreet enquiries about her as well as Clara Pilkington,' Petrie continued. 'I have a few contacts in London, including one in Scotland Yard. But I'll be surprised if there's anything to discover about that lady except that she's what we already know her to be: rich, with a strong sense of entitlement, and a very thick skin. It's hard to see what her motive would be. I very much doubt she needs more money than she already has.'

He laughed. 'And I can't imagine there's a clandestine romance involved. I suspect we've drawn a blank this time, de Silva. Never mind, the game's not over yet. We have other people to see. For the present, I'd better not neglect my social engagements in case it arouses comment. But I suggest you speak to Canon Ryder next.

CHAPTER 10

'As you can tell, William Petrie certainly doesn't mince his words in my presence now,' said de Silva when he came to the end of recounting the interview to Jane.

They sat in the sunshine as the afternoon drew to its close. A hum of voices and laughter came from some couples playing a game of quoits further along the deck. Other passengers watched, some of them taking shots of the play with their cameras. It reminded de Silva that his own hadn't come out of its case since they had gone ashore at Bombay.

'Perhaps he doesn't see you as a subordinate any longer.'

'I hardly think so.'

'He and Lady Caroline were very welcoming last night. They didn't need to invite us if they hadn't wanted to. I think they're different from Archie and Florence – more liberal in their outlook – certainly Lady Caroline is.'

'I thought you liked Archie and Florence.'

'Oh, I do, and at heart, I think you do too; even if they do drive you mad sometimes.'

De Silva chuckled. 'I suppose I do. When you get to know them better, they both have good qualities.'

'Well then, who's next?'

'The canon, George Ryder. Petrie wants me to see him alone. He's concerned that if he's too often absent from his social engagements, it will start to raise suspicion.'

'If everyone on the ship is as acute as Mrs Pilkington, I'm afraid there may be speculation anyway,' said Jane.

'Let's hope they're not.'

'And after Canon Ryder?'

'Mrs March and her fiancé. And after that, we have the romantic novelist.' He grinned. 'It's a pity she doesn't write detective stories, or she might be a help.' He squeezed Jane's hand. 'But thankfully, I have someone who reads them.'

The deck quoits players must have finished their match for they were shaking hands and gathering up their equipment. It was time to dress for dinner. De Silva stood up and offered Jane his arm.

Strolling along the deck in the direction of their cabin, the fast-ebbing light was changing the cobalt-blue sea to indigo, and the sky was a haze of lilac and pink that deepened to crimson on the horizon as the sun set.

'Let's stay and watch the sun go down,' said Jane.

Arm in arm, they leant against the rail. Again, de Silva thought of his camera, sat on the bedside table in their cabin. But there would be little point in fetching it; a sunset photographed in black and white would be a pale reflection of the real thing.

The sea and sky seemed to hold their breath, then with the suddenness that was so characteristic of the tropics, the dark waters swallowed the fiery disc.

'Beautiful,' said Jane. 'When they're so spectacular, I don't think I'll ever tire of watching sunsets.'

'Neither will I.'

He frowned. 'I'm sorry that this holiday hasn't turned out quite as I planned.'

'It's hardly your fault, dear. Anyway, I'm relying on you to find the murderer by teatime tomorrow, then we needn't be troubled any longer.'

He laughed. 'I'm afraid I may not be able to live up to your expectations.'

'Poor Mr Pashley. I shouldn't treat his death so lightly. I suppose there must be someone who will mourn him.'

'At the moment, there doesn't seem to be a queue.'

'Lady Caroline was telling me that as well as the articles he wrote for *The Monocle*, he'd published a number of very scurrilous diaries. That kind of thing doesn't tend to make a person popular.'

De Silva frowned. 'It does puzzle me where Pashley's money came from. The clothes and other possessions I found in his cabin were all very high quality and must have been expensive. Your favourite novelist, Mrs Christie, may make a lot of money from her detective stories, but I believe she's the exception.'

'Did Captain McDowell have any information about who was to be notified back in England?'

'Only Pashley's housekeeper and his solicitor. He owned a flat in a part of London called Chelsea.'

'That's a popular area for artists and writers, but not all that expensive, so his fancy possessions may be deceptive. Perhaps he had family money, or one of the newspapers he wrote for helped with his fare and expenses. After all, they'd want him in Cabin Class.'

'Very true.'

'What's been done with his body?'

'It's being kept in the ship's clinic until Captain McDowell decides what to do with it. Now, I think that we both deserve a good dinner and some dancing this evening.'

'That would be lovely. I saw on the ship's programme that Harry Delaney and his band are playing for us again tonight.'

'Then let's forget about Charles Pashley for a few hours and enjoy ourselves.'

CHAPTER 11

The following morning, de Silva sent a message to George Ryder's cabin, but the steward returned, saying Ryder wasn't there.

'The steward on duty on the corridor thinks he often goes to the chapel, sir,' the man said. 'Shall I look for him there?'

'No, I'll go myself.'

It was the first time that de Silva had entered the ship's chapel, although Jane had been to a service. For a moment, he took in the quiet beauty of the dark panelling and well-polished pews. Four elegant brass chandeliers hung from the ceiling. The two furthest from the entrance illuminated the intricate ironwork of the altar rail and the richly embroidered red and gold altar cloth. Above the altar hung a large painting of Jesus ascending to Heaven in the company of angels. The smell of incense made de Silva's nose prickle.

There was a creak; someone was getting up from one of the pews towards the front. He wore a dark suit and a dog collar. 'Good morning,' he said. 'Do you need any help?'

De Silva suppressed the urge to recoil. One side of the man's face was horribly scarred, the skin puckered and raw from the corner of his left eye to his jawline. De Silva wondered if it was an injury he had received in the war. He must be in his late forties, so he could easily have seen active service.

'I'm looking for Canon Ryder.'

'Then you've found him. May I ask to whom I have the pleasure of speaking?'

'My name is de Silva.'

Ryder closed his prayer book and walked back down the aisle to where de Silva stood. As he did so, the light from one of the chandeliers fell on his sleeve, highlighting a smattering of something rust coloured. Briskly, he rubbed it away.

'I fear that the maintenance of this chapel leaves something to be desired. I'm afraid the ship's cleaners don't place the house of God very high on their list of duties. But forgive me, I'm wasting your time with my mundane complaints. What can I do for you?'

'You may already be aware that one of the passengers, Charles Pashley, died of a heart attack early yesterday morning. As I'm an inspector in the Royal Ceylon Police and happened to be travelling on the ship, Captain McDowell and Mr William Petrie, the government agent for the Central Province in Ceylon, who's also on board, have asked me to assist in sorting the sad business out.'

'Ah, I see. As you say, a sad business. The gentleman's cabin was very close to mine, although I was attending an early service here on the morning he was found, so only heard of his death later. I believe he was travelling alone, and there was no grieving member of the family who might have welcomed a visit. In any case, it's not for me to interfere with the ship's chaplain's pastoral duties; unless, of course, he requests my assistance.'

'Can you remember when you last saw Mr Pashley?'

Ryder pondered a moment. 'It was at dinner. He was seated at a table close to mine. I shared a table with two couples who've been attending chapel regularly – if you wish, I can give you their names.'

'Thank you, but that won't be necessary for the moment.'

'I don't recall seeing Pashley again after dinner ended. I retired to bed a little before eleven o'clock and didn't meet him in the corridor on the way to my cabin.'

His chest heaved with a series of rasping coughs. 'My apologies,' he croaked as the fit subsided. 'My lungs are weak.'

'I'm sorry to hear that, sir. I won't detain you long, but as your cabin was close to Mr Pashley's, we'd be interested in knowing anything you might be able to tell us about him.'

'I'm afraid there's nothing. You may find that surprising as we were close neighbours on the ship, but I doubt Charles Pashley had any time for a humble priest like myself. I understand from Mrs Meadows, who comes regularly to services, that in London, he moves in exalted circles. Our interests and experiences would have been worlds apart. We exchanged the usual civilities if we met in the corridor, but that was all.'

'Did you notice him having many visitors to his cabin?'

Ryder frowned. 'I couldn't say for certain whether he had any, but if he did, I was never disturbed by their comings and goings. Inspector, I hope you don't mind my asking, but what is the point of these questions? Has there been any suggestion of foul play?'

'Nothing of that kind,' said de Silva quickly. He feared his last question had been too blunt. 'We're merely trying to piece together a picture of how Mr Pashley spent his time on the ship. Very little seems to be known about his personal life. If he had become friendly with anyone who might know any details of it, it might prevent us from overlooking friends or relations who would be distressed by not being told of his death.'

The mild expression on Ryder's face indicated that he accepted the explanation. He appeared to be more easily satisfied than Mrs Pilkington.

'May I ask how you passed the time between dinner and retiring to bed on the night Mr Pashley died?'

'I spent about an hour here. I like to have a period of private prayer and reflection before I retire for the night. Then I went to my cabin and got ready for bed. I read for a short while before turning off the light and sleeping.'

Clearing his throat, he rubbed a thumb over the spine of his prayer book and frowned. 'Inspector, are you sure there isn't something you're not telling me?'

'Nothing, I assure you, sir. As I say, it's just for the record.' De Silva dislike lying, but for now, he seemed to have very little choice.

'Then if there's nothing else I can help you with, I'll return to my cabin.'

'Of course. I'm sorry to have kept you. Thank you for your help.'

* * *

'I know who you mean,' said Jane when de Silva told her about his meeting with Ryder and the canon's scars. 'We were both in a group of people talking to the ship's chaplain after the Sunday service before we reached Bombay, but I didn't catch his name then. He seemed very quiet and gentlemanly. I'm sure he'd be horrified if he thought he was a suspect.'

'Plenty of killers have hidden their dark side under a cloak of inoffensiveness,' said de Silva grimly. 'Think of Dr Crippen.'

'That's true, but I very much doubt Canon Ryder is one of them. And how dreadful to have to live with those terrible scars. I wonder where the poor man got them. In the war, do you think?'

'I assume so. He looks old enough.'

She sighed and smoothed out the piece of embroidery she was working on.

'I hope I'm not going to run out of magenta silk before I've finished these flowers. I wonder if there'll be shops in Cairo where one can buy that sort of thing.' She rested her chin on her hand. 'Or perhaps there won't be many shops, just markets with local crafts and delicious food. Rather like the bazaar in Nuala but much bigger.'

She looked at him quizzically. 'You're not really listening, are you, dear?'

'Sorry.'

'It's alright. I know it's difficult to think about anything apart from your case.'

She put her embroidery aside. 'Why don't we go to the lounge? It would be nice to have a cold drink before lunch. Maybe you should look for William Petrie afterwards. He might have heard something from London that will help. It's rather soon, but I suppose it's possible.'

He stood up. 'Yes, a cold ginger beer would be very welcome.' He offered her his arm. 'Shall we?'

The main lounge in Tourist Class buzzed with conversation and laughter. Sunlight streamed through the large picture windows. De Silva and Jane found a free table and ordered their drinks from a white-jacketed steward. They didn't have to wait long; as the cool liquid slipped down his throat, de Silva felt a little more at peace with the world.

'Good day to you!'

He looked up and saw the smiling faces of James Ross and his wife, Barbara. 'Ginger beer, what an excellent idea. May we join you?' Ross asked jovially.

'We'd be delighted,' Jane said with a smile.

'Poor Barbara was suffering from one of her headaches yesterday,' Ross went on. 'We didn't do much.'

'I told James I would be perfectly alright on my own in our cabin, but he insisted on staying with me.'

Her husband grinned. 'You know I don't want to let you out of my sight since you got so lost the other day.'

Barbara laughed awkwardly. 'I do have the most terrible sense of direction. I ended up in a laundry cupboard.'

'I hope you're feeling better today, ma'am,' said de Silva.

'Oh, I'm perfectly fine, thank you. I think I just had too much sun. It was so lovely being out on deck and enjoying the scenery. The colours of the sea and the sky are so wonderful, don't you think? I'm afraid we shall have to get used to cold weather when we arrive in England. It might even be snowing.'

De Silva drank his ginger beer, smiling and nodding as Barbara Ross rattled on. She was a pleasant woman, but she did talk a great deal, and if he'd been asked afterwards what she was talking about, he couldn't have given a sensible answer. He was far too preoccupied with thoughts of the investigations he had made so far and those that were still to come.

Jane gave him a surreptitious dig in the ribs as they followed the Rosses into the dining room. 'Shanti, you're still miles away,' she whispered. 'Do try to forget about Charles Pashley for a little while.'

De Silva sighed. 'I'll do my best.'

The meal began with tomato soup. He raised the first spoonful to his lips with very little optimism, but the flavour was better than he had expected. The choice of main dish included vegetable curry which he knew from a previous evening was not bad. He chose that and, while the four of them waited to be served, made small talk with the Rosses about their plans on their return to England.

The food arrived, borne by stewards with white napkins over their arms. When they had withdrawn, James Ross stabbed a fork into his plate of lamb hotpot. 'How's the photography coming on, de Silva?'

'James must have used up dozens of films since we came on board at Hong Kong,' said his wife.

'Not quite dozens, dear, but the ship's photographer is

developing some of the ones I have taken. If they haven't turned out well, I'll probably do more. The bright sunlight shining on the white paint of the superstructure can cause problems with overexposure. I'd be delighted to take anything along for you, de Silva. The chap's very obliging and not terribly busy. I think the novelty of having their photographs taken on board ship has worn off for many people by now.'

'That would be kind. I have finished a roll of film.'

'Just tell one of the stewards to drop it into my cabin.'

'Thank you, I will.'

There was a commotion at the far end of the restaurant, and heads turned. A man had stumbled into one the tables. He righted himself and before anyone could remonstrate, hurried on, leaving chaos behind him. A stout man sat at the table jumped up; red wine stained his shirt front. One of his lady companions looked down with dismay at the splashes of lamb gravy on the bodice of her dress.

The author of the disaster was already halfway to the restaurant's double doors when an older man who was sat at a table near the de Silvas' caught him by the wrist as he passed and spun him round. 'For God's sake, man!' de Silva heard the older man bark. 'What d'you think you're playing at? Go back and apologise at once.'

The younger man – de Silva recognised him now as Harry Delaney, the singer with the band that they had danced to on the previous evenings – scowled, then dragging his feet, returned to the table he had knocked into.

'Extraordinary behaviour,' said James Ross. 'Isn't that fellow the singer? He'll be lucky if there's no complaint to the captain. If he doesn't watch his step, I expect he'll find himself eating in the crew's quarters in future.'

Looking at Delaney's flushed, handsome face and resentful expression as he passed their table and headed once more for the double doors, de Silva wondered what had caused the American to behave so badly. Ross was right; the captain was likely to be severely displeased if it came to his attention that passengers had been upset. What had happened to make Delaney careless as to whether he lost a privilege? If it hadn't been early in the day, de Silva would have thought he was drunk.

The stout gentleman and his lady companion stalked from the restaurant, apparently not much placated by Delaney's apology. The hum of conversation, the chink of glasses, and the soft clatter of cutlery was restored. Barbara Ross took a sip of her Elephant ginger beer. 'These theatrical people can be very eccentric,' she remarked. 'I had a schoolfriend who went on the stage. She dyed her hair platinum blonde and ran off to Brighton with a married man. It was quite a scandal.'

James Ross spluttered into his glass. 'I don't think *that* woman is a suitable subject for conversation, Barbara.'

His wife smiled sweetly. 'If you say not, dear.'

De Silva concealed his amusement. Barbara was obviously a lot less stuffy than her husband. Despite her being a mite too talkative for his taste, he decided that he liked her.

He said as much to Jane when, lunch over, they were walking back to their cabin for a nap.

'I like them both,' she said, then lowered her voice. 'Although at the risk of being unkind, I suspect James Ross drinks more than he should.'

'What makes you say that?'

'Just an impression I have. I once met Barbara on deck, and we had a little time alone. You were busy with William Petrie. She hinted she and her husband argued a lot. I suspect that may be the cause of her frequent "headaches". All the same, I agree that they're good company.'

As he unlocked the cabin door, de Silva felt a twinge of guilt for Jane. Apart from the Rosses, not many people on the ship had even passed the time of day with them. Back in Nuala, there had been difficult occasions at first, but now there were very few people who didn't accept they were a couple.

When one left home only infrequently, it was easy to forget that Nuala wasn't the world. Correspondingly, it was hard to ignore that, on this ship, there had been numerous disapproving looks. He'd been distracted by the work Pashley's murder entailed and able to put those looks out of his mind, but for Jane it must be harder to put up with. Not for the first time, he worried that he had been unfair asking her to marry him.

'What is it? Have I said something wrong?' she asked as he stood aside to let her walk in.

'No, it's what you didn't say – that there are plenty of people on the ship with whom we wouldn't be comfortable; nor would they welcome our company.'

She sighed. 'I'm afraid that's true. But are they people you care about? I know I don't.'

'No, I'm only concerned it might upset you.'

'Then don't be.'

He heard a crackle and realised that he'd stepped on a note that had been slipped under the door.

'Who's it from?' she asked, stifling a yawn. 'Oh dear, this sea air is really very enervating.'

'I'm afraid I'll have to do without that nap,' said de Silva scanning the lines written in Petrie's bold handwriting. 'William Petrie wants to see me.'

He reached for her hand. 'Are you sure you have no regrets?'

She kissed his cheek. 'I'm surprised you need to ask. Now, go and see Mr Petrie and try not to let him keep you too long.'

* * *

He found Petrie in the Cabin Class bar; he stood up as de Silva approached.

'I trust you've had lunch?'

'I have, thank you, sir.'

Petrie gestured to the glass on the table. 'Will you have a whisky?'

'A small one, thank you.'

Raising his arm, Petrie clicked his fingers, pointed at his glass and then at de Silva. The steward whose attention he had caught hurried off in the direction of the bar.

'Made any progress with Ryder?'

'I've interviewed him, sir. He claims he spoke rarely with Pashley and knew very little about him apart from the fact that Pashley moved in different social circles and would probably have had no time for him.'

'Did you get the feeling Ryder resented that?'

'Not at all. He seemed a mild-mannered, self-effacing type.'

'What was his account of how he spent the evening?'

Briefly, de Silva explained then they fell silent as the steward brought the whisky.

'We'll leave Ryder aside for the moment,' said Petrie when the man had gone. He stared down into his glass and swirled the inch of whisky left in it. De Silva swallowed a mouthful of his own. It was a fine single malt. Petrie was obviously more of a connoisseur than Archie Clutterbuck.

A group came to sit at the table nearby, and Petrie drained his glass. 'If you're ready, I suggest we take a turn on deck.'

With regret, de Silva drank up quickly and followed Petrie's tall figure as he strode out of the bar.

'I'm sorry about that,' he said when they reached the deck and had found a quiet spot. 'Some people have sharp ears, eh?'

'Indeed, they do.'

'We can't be too careful.'

He lit a cigarette and leant on the rail, staring out to sea. 'Two down, four to go,' he remarked. 'I suggest the two of us tackle Chiltern and Mrs March together. I'd like you to interview the Meadows woman without her employer present, just to make sure she has nothing to add that might help us. We can decide about Mrs de Vere later.'

'Have you heard anything from your contacts in London yet, sir?'

'Not yet, but I hope to soon. I don't think we need worry about that. We still have a long way to travel before anyone can leave the ship. It's turned out to be a blessing we won't be calling at Aden.'

A commotion by one of the stairways leading onto the deck drew their attention. A lady of mature years, attended by a small army of stewards carrying her rugs, books and refreshments, had appeared. She was dressed in a flowing, chiffon garment in woodland shades. A green sunhat with an extravagantly wide brim sat atop an abundance of burnished copper hair that would not have been out of place in a Pre-Raphaelite painting. She proceeded to take an inordinate amount of time deciding where she wanted her steamer chair positioned and, on each occasion, no sooner had she decided than she changed her mind again.

Petrie observed the party. 'Ah, I believe that's Mrs de Vere now, our lady novelist whom we haven't interviewed yet. Lady Caroline pointed her out to me at a reception that Captain McDowell gave in Cabin Class one evening before Pashley died. Poor fellows,' he went on as the stewards lugged the lady's impedimenta to yet another spot. 'I'd be tempted to throw the lot overboard and her with it.'

De Silva was taken aback. This was a new side to William Petrie. He was unexpectedly adopting some of his wife's nonchalance in the company of a subordinate.

A sudden shriek startled de Silva. Something had

thrown the nomadic little party into confusion; Mrs de Vere appeared to have been taken ill. De Silva wondered out loud if they should call for the ship's doctor.

Petrie shook his head. 'I'm sure the stewards will deal with whatever's necessary. She looks to me to be unharmed. It's one of her bearers who has injured himself in the process of moving her steamer chair.'

The steward did indeed look to have injured his hand which was bleeding profusely, perhaps from a sharp splinter. As far as de Silva could tell, the man took his injury stoically, whereas the novelist was giving a performance worthy of Sarah Bernhardt. She was obviously fond of creating a drama, but some people did have a horror of blood. De Silva recalled one of his constables in Colombo who had struggled with the inconvenient affliction.

Venetia de Vere quietened. Fortunately, she hadn't noticed them, so Petrie and de Silva turned their attention back to the sea. Outlined against the azure sky, and about half a mile away, another cruise ship steamed past them in the opposite direction. Its elegant, white silhouette gleamed in the sun. In another direction, the lower lines and blacker smoke of two more ships suggested that they were freighters.

'*Quinquireme of Ninevah from distant Ophir,*' quoted Petrie.

'*Rowing home to haven in sunny Palestine,*
With a cargo of ivory,
And apes and peacocks…'

He paused. 'Once, I had it by heart,' he said glumly.

'*Sandalwood, cedarwood, and sweet white wine,*' supplied de Silva.

Petrie looked surprised. 'You know John Masefield's work?' He gave de Silva an apologetic smile. 'I'm sorry, there's no reason why you shouldn't. We learnt some of his poems at school, where I was not, I'm afraid, a very attentive pupil, but since then, Lady Caroline has taught me to enjoy poetry.'

De Silva smiled. 'As I expect you know, in Ceylon, our education follows the British model, but like you, I have my wife to thank for my appreciation of the books I read very reluctantly in those days.'

'And what's your opinion of the British system?'

De Silva searched for the right words. 'It has many benefits,' he said at last.

'Very diplomatic.' Petrie's face cracked into a mischievous grin that again took de Silva by surprise. 'I imagine not all of your countrymen feel that.' The grin faded. 'The world is changing, my friend. Throughout history, no empire has lasted forever, and at home, events in Germany are causing concern. This man Hitler has his admirers, but in my view, their faith in him is misplaced.'

He tossed the end of his cigarette into the waves. 'Enough politics. Do you remember how the poem goes on?'

De Silva racked his brains.

'*Stately Spanish galleon coming from the Isthmus,*
Dipping through the Tropics by the palm-green shores…'

He stopped. 'Memory fails me too, sir. I think there's something about a cargo of Tyne coal and cheap tin trays.'

'I expect the ladies would finish it with no difficulty.' Petrie's brow furrowed. 'Stick to what we do best, eh, de Silva? We need to get on with interviewing Chiltern and Mrs March. Our own version of the ape and the peacock.'

'Petrie!'

They both looked over their shoulders to see a balding man with a military-style moustache striding in their direction. 'An old acquaintance from my Colombo days in Government House,' Petrie muttered quickly. 'Shall we continue this conversation later?'

'Of course.'

De Silva hurried away before the balding man could reach them. It might have been awkward being introduced and possibly needing to deflect unwelcome questions. A pity. The conversation had been interesting. Unexpectedly, Petrie might be a man with whom one could risk having a frank exchange of views.

CHAPTER 12

'I didn't know where you'd got to.'

De Silva had been back in their cabin for an hour before Jane returned.

'Lady Caroline invited me to take tea with her.'

'And did you have an interesting conversation?'

'Yes, we did. She suggested that the murderer might be someone whose cabin's not on Pashley's corridor. She posed a good question: how would the present suspects drug Pashley? Is there evidence that any of them spent time alone with him to have the opportunity?'

'It's a fair point, and she's right. Unfortunately, it means we'd end up with a whole boatload of people to interview.'

He remembered Clara Pilkington's sleeping draught. That was the only obvious method of drugging someone that he'd heard of being to hand among Pashley's neighbours, but he couldn't imagine the two spending a convivial evening together.

'I'd like to start with the obvious suspects first though,' he went on. 'If the steward's lying, or negligent in his duties, I expect we'll find him out eventually.'

'How was your talk with William Petrie?'

'Interrupted by some fellow from Government House he's acquainted with. Not much has been decided.'

Jane sat down in one of the easy chairs and picked up her embroidery. 'Never mind. Unless they decide to swim, no one can leave the ship for the present.'

'William Petrie said much the same thing.'

'What did he say about Canon Ryder?'

'Very little, but he didn't say he wanted Ryder interviewed again either. Oh, and we saw Mrs de Vere, the novelist whose cabin is on Pashley's corridor.' He recounted the scene for Jane's amusement. 'After that, we talked about poetry.'

Jane put down her embroidery and shaded her eyes against the sun coming through the porthole. 'That must have surprised you.'

'It did. He quoted from John Masefield's *Cargoes*.'

'I like that one.'

'Me too, but I can't imagine Archie Clutterbuck coming out with it.'

'Neither can I. William Petrie seems to be of a different stamp to Archie. Lady Caroline isn't at all like Florence either.'

'Well,' said de Silva with a grin, 'I don't suppose many people are.'

CHAPTER 13

In the morning, they found a table for two in a quiet corner of the restaurant to have breakfast. De Silva wasn't in the mood for making polite conversation. He wanted to compose himself in readiness for the meeting with Diana March and her fiancé. While he waited for one of the stewards to come to take their order, he absent-mindedly rearranged the cutlery in front of him. Jane put her hand on his. 'Do try to relax, dear. I'm sure it will go far better than you expect.'

'I hope you're right.'

She picked up the menu and studied it. 'I'm sure I am. Oh good, grilled kippers. I think I'll have some.'

After breakfast, they returned to their cabin to find a note from William Petrie. He had arranged the meeting with Diana March and Arthur Chiltern for eleven o'clock.

'I think I'll stay here and read my book for a while,' said Jane. 'The forecast is for a very hot day. What are you going to do while you wait, dear?'

'I'll feel better for some exercise. A turn or two round the deck should do the trick.'

Out on deck, there was no one about. He completed two brisk circuits then sat down on a deckchair in the shade. The forecast had been right; there wasn't a cloud in the sky and the deck shimmered in the heat. They were too far out from land for seagulls now. The only sounds were the flapping of a canvas cover that had worked loose from a stack of life rafts by the rails, the soft hiss of the ship cutting through the waves, and the underlying throb of the engines. Closing his eyes, he saw dancing pinpricks of green, yellow and red. The smell of salt mingled with the fainter aroma of engine oil and soot.

The sound of coughing disturbed his peace. He opened his eyes and realised that he wasn't alone. The tall man standing at the rail had his back to him, apparently unaware that he was awake. Even from behind, he looked tense, his shoulders hunched and his jacket taut across his back. De Silva saw a plume of cigarette smoke rise, then the man dropped the stub and ground it under his heel before knocking it into the sea with the side of his shoe. He turned abruptly, and his glance crossed with de Silva's. It was Harry Delaney. He flinched and gave an awkward nod before hurrying away.

De Silva frowned. What troubled Delaney? Perhaps he should consider questioning him? But then what possible connection could there be between Delaney and Charles Pashley? The singer might be plagued by a variety of other troubles. He glanced at his watch and levered himself out of his deckchair. It was time to join Petrie.

* * *

Diana March's stateroom wasn't quite as grand as Mrs Pilkington's, but it was still very luxurious. As he went to sit down in the chair she indicated, his feet sank into thick-pile, cream carpet. The furniture was elegant but looked comfortable. On the wall opposite the entrance door, a magnificent mural composed of many different polished woods drew his attention. He recognised some of Ceylon's native ones – coromandel, satinwood, and ebony. The picture showed a ship, her sails unfurled as she beat against the wind under a sky full of scudding clouds.

He would have liked more time to study the mural, but Diana March was speaking, and he must turn his attention to what was being said. He noticed that between her and her fiancé, she was by far the more composed of the two. Now he saw them both more closely than he had at the dinner with the Petries in Cabin Class, de Silva guessed that she was the elder by a few years, perhaps in her mid-thirties.

Arthur Chiltern stood by one of the windows, his hand resting on the back of an armchair. De Silva noticed how his small, bristly moustache accentuated his weak chin. He seemed content to leave the talking to his beloved and had suggested holding the meeting in her stateroom rather than his own.

Petrie made the introductions then asked after Arthur Chiltern's parents. 'I knew your father and mother quite well when I was in England,' he said. 'I hope they are both in good health.'

'I've been away for five years, but as far as I'm aware, they are,' said Chiltern, rather ungraciously to de Silva's mind.

Diana March cut in. 'How kind of you to ask, Mr Petrie.' Her smile transformed the air that de Silva had thought haughty when he first saw her. 'This is a dreadful business,' she went on. Her voice had a husky timbre. 'We were so looking forward to the cruise and to have a murder happen on our doorstep is most unpleasant.'

So, Mrs March and Chiltern already knew that Pashley had been murdered, thought de Silva.

William Petrie frowned. 'May I ask who told you that, Mrs March?'

'Mrs Pilkington. I hope she didn't speak out of turn. We've mentioned it to no one else. I expect the last thing that you and Captain McDowell want is a panic on the ship.'

'Indeed, we don't. Thank you.'

'Arthur and I would like to help. You must let us know if there's anything at all we can do.'

She smoothed down the skirt of her immaculately tailored, white dress. De Silva found it difficult to take his eyes off the long, slender legs clad in sheer silk stockings.

'Do you think it's likely the murderer will strike again?' she asked.

William Petrie cleared his throat. 'Extremely unlikely. Inspector de Silva and I believe that the culprit is someone with a grudge against Charles Pashley. He would have no reason to attack unless someone threatened him with exposure. For that reason, I can't impress upon you too strongly, that if you or your fiancé have even the faintest suspicion who may be the perpetrator of the crime, you do nothing to provoke them. We will take all necessary action.'

'That's very reassuring to hear.' Diana March smiled again. She rested her hand lightly on the arm of her chair. A ring set with one of the largest diamonds de Silva had ever seen set off her long, slim fingers; scarlet polish accentuated her flawless nails.

'Did you have occasion to speak to Mr Pashley often?' asked Petrie.

'Hardly a word passed between us.'

'The man was a bounder,' Chiltern butted in.

'That's a little harsh, my dear,' said Diana March in an admonishing tone. 'Let's not forget that we haven't really been courting new acquaintances on the voyage.' She bestowed one of her smiles on Chiltern, and his expression softened. For a moment, he looked almost boyish.

A door to one side of the room opened and a uniformed maid appeared. Several evening dresses embellished with embroidery and feathers were draped over her arm. Behind her, de Silva glimpsed a sumptuous bed, canopied with white muslin curtains.

The moment she saw her mistress had visitors, she

stopped. 'I'm sorry, madam,' she stuttered. 'The dresses need pressing, and I didn't know you had company this morning.'

'Never mind, Perkins. Get on with your work.'

The maid bobbed an awkward curtsey and scuttled out of the room.

'One of the inconveniences of life on board ship,' remarked Diana March as the door closed. 'Far less space and privacy than one is used to.'

De Silva couldn't help but reflect that there was many a home in Ceylon where even the largest of families would have thought that the gods smiled on them if they had accommodation as spacious as Mrs March's. Presumably Chiltern's stateroom next door was no less impressive.

'Did you notice any unusual noises on the night of Mr Pashley's death?' asked Petrie.

Diana March pondered for a few moments before shaking her head.

'What about you, Mr Chiltern?'

'None.'

'Do you recollect hearing altercations at any earlier times?'

Chiltern let out an impatient snort. 'Do you mean since we left Hong Kong? We have better things to do than listen at doors.'

'Can you tell me what your movements were last Wednesday evening?'

'Good God, sir,' exploded Chiltern. 'Are you accusing us of being involved?'

'Arthur, please…' Diana March intervened. 'I'm sure Mr Petrie doesn't think that.' She turned to Petrie. 'I expect you need to ask these questions to build up a picture of events on the night Mr Pashley died, don't you? It was the night he died I take it?'

'Thank you, Mrs March. We believe it was actually in the early hours of Thursday morning.'

'We had dinner at the captain's table, then danced for a while. We retired to bed – let me think, it must have been about two o'clock. In the morning I breakfasted in my room at ten before dressing. Arthur always goes to the restaurant for breakfast.' She smiled. 'I refuse to have his favourite kippers anywhere near my stateroom. Do you remember what time you went, Arthur?'

'Nine o'clock or thereabouts,' muttered Chiltern.

An awkward silence fell, broken by Diana March. 'I'm so sorry we can't be of more help to you, Mr Petrie.'

'It's no matter, Mrs March. But if you should recall anything, the inspector and I would be grateful if you would let us know.'

'Of course.'

Her eyes rested on de Silva. 'How fortuitous that you were on board, Inspector de Silva.'

'Purely in a private capacity. My wife and I are taking a holiday.'

'How delightful. Are you going all the way to England?'

'Port Said, then inland to visit the pyramids.'

'Oh, I should love to see the pyramids. I fear it will have to be another time though. Arthur and I are anxious to get to England. I'm longing to meet his family.'

'Have you been away for many years?' asked Petrie.

'I've never lived in England. This will be my first visit. My grandfather and my father had businesses in Shanghai, as did my late husband. I was born there.'

Out of the corner of his eye, de Silva saw Chiltern's bony fingers drum on the back of the armchair. 'Darling,' he said irritably, 'we've agreed to meet the Montagues for drinks before lunch.'

'Forgive us, Mr Petrie. Inspector de Silva.' Diana March held out a hand to each of them in turn. As he kissed it, de Silva smelt sandalwood. When he raised his head, he saw the warmth in her dark eyes. 'I hope,' she murmured, 'that our next meeting will be in more pleasant circumstances.'

* * *

'One almost feels sorry for her,' said Petrie. 'Granted she chose him, but I hope she'll never regret saddling herself with that dunderhead. There must have been plenty of men willing to marry her. It's impossible to credit that such a delightful creature would be involved in Pashley's murder.'

Not impossible, thought de Silva, but unlikely.

Petrie glanced at him. 'Surely you agree?'

'At this stage, sir, I never rule out anyone.'

He waited for a dressing down. If this had been Archie Clutterbuck, he would probably have got one. But, after a pause, William Petrie merely shrugged. 'I can't deny it's a valid point of view. But if Diana March is our murderer, I'll eat my hat.'

* * *

'How did it go?' Jane studied her reflection in the dressing table mirror. After Diana March's suite, the room felt to de Silva like a doll's house.

She picked up a puff and dabbed powder on her cheeks then frowned. 'Oh, dear, I think I caught the sun yesterday. I see a few freckles.'

'I can't see any, my love,' said de Silva absently.

'That's because you're not looking.'

She gave him a sympathetic glance. 'Were you disappointed with the interview?'

'I suppose I shouldn't be,' he said reluctantly. 'Murder's rarely an easy case to solve.'

Jane applied a touch of pink to her lips. 'That's the spirit. Anyway, you haven't spoken to everyone whose cabin is on the same corridor as Pashley's yet.'

'That's true. So, what did you get up to while I was away?'

'Well, I've had an interesting morning. I grew tired of being in the cabin, so I went up on deck, but it was so dreadfully hot that I decided to read in one of the lounges instead.

'It was almost deserted there. Most people were probably resting in their cabins. I felt sorry for the lady from the entertainments crew, playing the piano with hardly anyone to hear her. She had such a lovely, light touch on the keys. I listened while she played my favourite Chopin *Nocturne*, and when she'd finished, I went over to thank her. She said her session was over, so I asked if she'd like to have a cup of tea with me. She said that she'd love to, and we had a most illuminating conversation.'

'Do you mean from the point of view of the case?'

She put her head on one side and thought for a moment. 'Not precisely,' she continued. 'But it might provide an insight into one of your suspects.'

'I'm intrigued. Carry on.'

'At first, the pianist, her name's Betty Falconer by the way, told me how she came to be on the cruise, but then we went on to talk about the other musicians she works with. She likes most of them, but she says that the American singer, Harry Delaney, is very temperamental.'

'I could have told you that from the way he behaved in the bazaar and in the dining room the other evening.'

'Yes, but there's more. Betty says that one of the passengers is obsessed with him, and that's what she thinks is making him even more irritable than usual.'

De Silva's brow furrowed. 'Did she say who it was?'

'No, and I didn't want to ask her to be indiscreet. But she did tell me it was a wealthy, older woman who was travelling alone in Cabin Class.'

'Do you think she meant Venetia de Vere?'

'She's the first one to spring to mind.'

'But how would they have met?'

'Apparently, it's the practice on the ship for the male entertainers to take their turn to act as dancing partners for unattached lady passengers, particularly the wealthy ones in Cabin Class. Being rather romantic looking, Harry Delaney's always in demand.'

'I'll have to think about this. Right now, I don't see a connection.' He put his arms around her waist and rested his chin on her shoulder. 'May I say that you're looking very lovely today?'

'You may; I thought I'd make an extra effort.'

An alarming thought jumped into his mind. Had he forgotten an anniversary?

Jane gave him a mischievous smile. 'No, you haven't forgotten anything. It's just that there's going to be a dancing competition this afternoon.'

'Are you expecting me to enter?'

'Well, I can't dance without a partner.'

'I suppose not.'

She turned her head to kiss him. 'It will be fun. You'll see.'

* * *

As he and Jane entered the lounge where the dancing competition was to be held, he saw that the area reserved for the orchestra was festooned with coloured streamers and bunches of balloons. Looking round the tables pushed back against the walls, Jane noticed the Rosses waving, and they went to join them.

'Isn't this fun!' said Barbara Ross. 'I love dancing.'

She tucked her hand into the crook of her husband's arm. 'James has been grumbling, but I know he'll enjoy it once we get started. Do you dance much at home?' She directed the question to both de Silva and Jane.

'Whenever we get the chance,' answered Jane. 'Some of the hotels in Nuala hold regular dances, and there's a dance hall too. But we've never entered a competition before.'

Barbara Ross beamed. 'I'm sure you'll do terribly well.'

She fanned herself with the pretty fan she held. It was of Indian design and the carmines, ochres and ultramarines had a silky sheen to them.

'What a lovely fan,' said Jane.

'James bought it for me in the market in Bombay.' She squeezed his arm, but only received a fleeting smile for her pains. 'Have you had a nice morning?' she asked, with what de Silva thought was rather forced brightness. He let Jane reply. It would hardly be appropriate to divulge the events of his day so far.

A flurry of activity in the area reserved for the band brought an end to the conversation. De Silva looked across and saw that the musicians had begun to take their places. The Master of Ceremonies arrived. A dapper man with heavily pomaded black hair, he made a great business of adjusting his microphone. When he tapped it with his knuckles to test it, it gave off a series of loud whistles and crackles.

'I think I'll go to the powder room before they begin,' said Jane.

Barbara Ross snapped her fan shut. 'I'll come too.'

After the ladies had departed, James Ross was not much more talkative than before. De Silva wondered what had happened to put him out of countenance. Whatever it was, it was possible he had already resorted to alcohol to console himself; the malty smell of whisky lingering about him was very noticeable.

Jane and Barbara Ross returned, and the Master of Ceremonies, finally satisfied with his microphone, announced the first dance.

'How will they decide who's won?' de Silva asked Jane as they took their places.

'I understand it will be by process of elimination.'

He grinned. 'We'd better survive a few rounds then. The honour of Nuala is at stake. Luckily, I think I can just about manage this first one.'

'I should hope so. We've danced the foxtrot dozens of times.'

'Slow, slow, quick, quick… is that it?'

'Full marks.'

'I think that went rather well,' he said when the music stopped, and he had time to catch his breath.

'There. I told you it wouldn't be difficult. I wonder what they'll play now?'

The MC announced a waltz, and de Silva felt relieved. It was a dance he could cope with quite easily. The opening bars of Johann Strauss' famous tune stole through the room. Although he had never seen them, de Silva liked the idea of the rolling, blue waters of the Danube that the music evoked. He pictured Viennese ballrooms where couples whirled past in ever-changing patterns of colours, like the kaleidoscope he had played with as a child.

'By the way,' he said as he and Jane danced. 'Do you have any idea what's wrong with James Ross this afternoon?'

'Oh, Barbara told me in the powder room that it was just a silly argument they had earlier. She thought she'd left her book on deck, but when he went to find it for her, it was gone. Then she remembered she'd been sitting in a different place altogether. It made them late for lunch, and he was cross.'

Steering Jane into what he hoped was a graceful twirl, de Silva raised an eyebrow. 'Late for lunch. What a disaster!'

'You might think that yourself if you were hungry!'

'Very true.'

He chuckled. 'I must say, Barbara Ross does seem rather scatter-brained. Between losing her way and losing her possessions, poor old Ross might have to tie a luggage label to her before he loses her altogether.'

Jane laughed. 'It's so nice to see you cheerful again.'

'Do you mean I haven't been?'

'You know you haven't, but I understand, and I did have some inkling of what I was getting into when I married a policeman.'

'Has it been as bad as all that?'

She smiled. 'Not bad at all. Now, we must concentrate, or we might be out at the end of this dance.'

'I'd say we acquitted ourselves very well,' he remarked when they sat down. The jitterbug had proved to be their undoing. They had only danced it once before in Nuala, and the band had taken the music at a brisk pace.

'Never mind. I'll be glad to sit out for a while. A cold drink would be nice.'

'Good idea. What would you like?'

'Barbara Ross says the bar stewards make a delicious cocktail from pineapple and mango juice with some rum and a dash of Angostura Bitters.'

'In the afternoon? It sounds very potent.'

'I'm sure we'd be safe with one.'

'Oh, why not? After all, we are on holiday.'

A passing steward took their order, and they settled down to watch the dancers who remained in the competition. Among them were the Rosses.

'He looks to be in a better mood now,' observed Jane.

'Probably because he thinks they might win.'

'For her sake, I hope they do.'

'Not for his too?'

Their cocktails arrived, and the steward set them down along with a small bowl of salted cashew nuts then went away. Jane took a sip. 'Mm, delicious.'

De Silva tried his own drink and nodded. 'Not bad.' He tossed a cashew into his mouth. 'You didn't tell me why you only want the Rosses to win for her sake.'

'Silly really, but I have the impression he's a difficult

man to live with. Barbara mentioned he can be very critical about little things, and she seemed upset.'

'Well, they look perfectly happy together now.'

'Yes, I suppose they do.'

Perhaps, de Silva thought as he watched the couple going through their paces in the next dance – an energetic affair called the Lindy Hop, invented to commemorate the flight of the aviator, Charles Lindberg from New York to Paris – the Rosses were the kind of couple who thrived on arguments. He remembered several colleagues in his days in the Colombo force who appeared to quarrel frequently with their wives. Their excuse was the pressures of policing the big city. It had been a major reason in his decision to move to Nuala. He hadn't wanted that life for him and Jane.

He had intended to forget the case for a while, but Jane was happy watching the dancing, so he let his mind wander in the direction that tempted it. He recalled George Ryder's mild, diffident manner; Arthur Chiltern's aristocratic irritability, and Diana March's charm. None of them were obvious choices for the murderer, but in a few days' time, would he think differently?

A round of applause brought him out of his reverie. Only two couples remained on the floor. One of them was the Rosses, and James Ross was smiling.

CHAPTER 14

'Damn the wretched woman! Doesn't she understand I have a ship to run? First Charles Pashley goes and gets himself killed. And now, that novelist woman throws herself into a fit of the vapours.'

Captain McDowell's grizzled beard quivered with indignation. He had called de Silva and Petrie to see him the next morning.

'And at dinner last night, I sat next to the Pilkington woman and had great difficulty keeping her quiet on the subject of Charles Pashley.' McDowell scowled. 'Was it really necessary to tell her, Petrie?'

'Couldn't be avoided, I'm afraid.'

'How many people know about Pashley now? Too many, I suppose. Once rumours start flying, one's lost the battle. It's a bad situation. Sailors are a superstitious lot, and a corpse on board ship is unlucky. I don't want a mutiny on my hands.'

'It may come to the point that making a statement does more to allay people's fears than saying nothing,' said Petrie. 'But I think we can wait a little longer. I'd prefer to be able to tell the passengers that the culprit has been found.'

'Quite.'

Petrie turned to de Silva. 'In any case, we can make ourselves useful and visit Mrs de Vere. It will give us an excuse to talk to her. We would have needed to do so anyway as her stateroom is on the same corridor as Pashley's. Do you know what's caused the trouble, McDowell?'

'Some problem with one of the crew, I believe.' He grunted. 'Grateful to you for dealing with it, Petrie.'

'Lady Caroline has filled me in a bit more on Venetia de Vere and her work,' said Petrie after they had parted company with the captain and were making their way back to the Cabin Class area of the ship. 'Apparently, she's written over two hundred books, all in a romantic vein. They sell like the proverbial hot cakes, so she must have made a very satisfactory living out of them.'

Since she could afford to travel Cabin Class, de Silva imagined that she had.

'She's been in Hong Kong and Singapore because she was invited to talk to various ladies' literary societies,' Petrie went on. He grinned. 'Best foot forward, eh? We'll have to do our utmost to smooth over whatever's upset the lady. I fear that if she won't be placated and McDowell gets dragged into it after all, he may spontaneously combust. He already has enough to deal with. One of the main engines is malfunctioning. The engineers are working on it, but you may have noticed that the ship hasn't been making as good headway as usual since yesterday. McDowell may need to arrange a place on a later convoy to go through the canal at Suez.'

* * *

Venetia de Vere wore pastel pink with cascades of ruffles. The diamond bracelet circling her wrist was so extravagant that de Silva wondered whether the stones were imitation. If not, it was clearly time that he tried to persuade Jane to bend her talents to writing romance.

In the muted light of the morning sun, her stateroom's

drawing room was also pastel-coloured, with lilac uphol-stery, a dove-grey carpet, and assorted bowls and vases of lusciously scented pink flowers. De Silva banished the thought that it would only take a sprinkling of powdered sugar to complete his feeling that he sat in a massive box of rose-flavoured Turkish Delight. From the agitated expres-sion on Mrs de Vere's heavily made-up face, he and Petrie had a delicate task ahead of them.

They barely had time to introduce themselves before she interrupted. 'I expected Captain McDowell.'

'He sends his apologies. Unfortunately, his duties make his absence unavoidable. I hope Inspector de Silva and I will be able to help.'

'I hope so too, Mr Petrie. This voyage has turned out to be most unsatisfactory. First, I was obliged to accept inside accommodation. They told me nothing else was left in Cabin Class. Now I've been insulted by one of the crew. I insist something be done.'

Mrs de Vere glowered at them both. De Silva had the sensation that he was being inspected by an iceberg. She might be a romantic novelist, but soft-hearted wasn't an appropriate adjective for her.

Petrie frowned. 'I'm sorry to hear that. Hopefully, there's been a misunderstanding, but can you tell us more about the circumstances?'

She shuddered. 'I can hardly bear to think of it. Suffice to say, that man, Delaney, had the temerity to lay a hand on me.' Her eyes narrowed. 'I'm surprised that the Blue Star Line employs a man who forgets his place. He should be dismissed and put ashore at the next available opportunity. I fail to understand why I've received no assurances it will be done.

'Furthermore,' she snapped, 'a valuable ring of mine has gone missing. A keepsake from my dear, departed husband. I shouldn't be surprised if it didn't turn up in the crew's quarters, but I suppose that's of little concern to Captain McDowell. He seems to think this business with Charles Pashley is more important than anything else.' She sniffed. 'Although it's hardly surprising someone wanted to kill Pashley.'

De Silva saw William Petrie give a start. As Captain McDowell said, they'd lost the battle.

'Oh, there's no need to look so dismayed, Mr Petrie,' she went on. 'You didn't think that murder could be kept secret for long, did you?'

'Regrettably, it seems that it can't. Did you know Charles Pashley well?'

Venetia de Vere's lips pursed in a moue of distaste. 'Better than I wished to. He was a thoroughly unpleasant individual. Oh, I willingly admit he had no time for me either. He made no bones about disliking my books. He had the nerve to describe them as trashy and trite. Why he thought that his nasty little columns, and his occasional attempts at writing plays – none of which survived for more than a few weeks in the West End – entitled him to style himself a literary critic, I failed to understand. He admitted that he dashed off his columns in a few minutes before he took his afternoon rest, then if any juicy piece of gossip emerged over dinner, he made whatever amendments were needed and gave the dispatch to the steward to send off early the next morning. Hardly a great practitioner of the literary craft.'

'When did you last speak to him?'

She paused a moment then shrugged. 'We wished each other a good evening and spoke briefly if we met on the way to dinner. One has to be civil.'

'We believe he was killed in the early hours of Thursday morning. May I ask what you were doing on Wednesday evening?'

'I dined at the captain's table then had coffee in the bar

with friends. I came to bed at about eleven o'clock. The steward will vouch for that.'

'Thank you. As you appear to have known Mr Pashley better than the other passengers in this part of the ship, may I ask if you can think of anyone who might have wished him dead?'

'Apart from myself?' She gave a tinkling laugh. 'My little joke. I deal in romance, not murder. I'm sure many people will be happy to know he's no longer polluting the air, but I can't help you with the name of the person who achieved that laudable result. If I could, I'd send them a bouquet.'

William Petrie cleared his throat. 'Thank you for your frankness, Mrs de Vere.'

'A pleasure, Mr Petrie. And you will make sure this man Delaney is dealt with, won't you? I insist it be treated as a matter of urgency.'

'Be assured, appropriate action will be taken.'

'I trust Harry Delaney won't be permitted to remain at large a moment longer to pester any other passengers.'

'That will be for the captain to decide.'

Venetia de Vere tossed her head. 'Well, I hope he comes to the right conclusion. And my ring needs to be recovered.'

'Is it possible that your maid misplaced it, ma'am?' ventured de Silva.

She glowered at him. 'Certainly not, and she's been with me for years. I trust her implicitly.'

'Very well,' said Petrie. 'Everything possible will be done.'

* * *

'What an impossible woman,' muttered Petrie as they walked away down the corridor. 'I don't know whether to believe her or not. Hard to say what motivated the complaint — the truth or vanity. And we're no further forward with the Pashley business,' he added gloomily.

De Silva had held back from mentioning what the pianist, Betty Falconer, had told Jane about Delaney, but he decided it was time to reveal it now.

As he explained how Jane had learnt from Betty Falconer that Harry Delaney claimed to be harassed by the importunate attentions of a wealthy female passenger in Cabin Class, William Petrie listened thoughtfully.

'Interesting,' he said when de Silva had finished. 'So, your supposition that the passenger might be Mrs de Vere seems to be correct. The question is, do we believe her story or Delaney's? It's credible that he would flatter a wealthy woman, either because his employers encourage it, or in the hope of some benefit to himself, but was he the one to step out of line, or did Mrs de Vere become an embarrassment? I suggest we keep this one under our hats for the moment, de Silva. We might question this Falconer woman officially, but it's likely to send more rumours flying round the ship. I'd rather avoid that for the present. Anyway, we need to speak to Harry Delaney himself now. If he sticks to a different story from Venetia de Vere's, McDowell will have a difficult decision to make. Unfortunately for Delaney, I doubt it will go his way. McDowell won't want any trouble, and Delaney is the more expendable of the two.'

They parted in the Cabin Class lobby, and de Silva started back to his cabin to find Jane. As he walked, Venetia de Vere's comment on how Pashley worked reminded him that when Pashley's body had been found, his next dispatch wasn't in his cabin. He must question the steward about that. After he'd found Pashley's body, why remove the dispatch? Had the murderer, whoever he or she was, had a reason for wanting to get rid of it? Or was it just that Pashley had departed from his customary pattern and not written anything that day?

He was still thinking about the possibilities when he reached their cabin. Jane looked up from her magazine and smiled a greeting.

'What did Captain McDowell want?'

He sat down in the armchair opposite her and rubbed a hand over his forehead. She listened while he told her about Venetia de Vere's accusations.

'If Betty Falconer's right,' she said when he had finished, 'far from pursuing her and taking liberties, Harry Delaney's probably desperate to extricate himself.'

'Hell has no fury like a woman scorned?'

'Yes. And if that's the case, I doubt she'll let the matter rest until he's sacked. What an awkward situation.'

'Fortunately, it's the captain who will eventually have to decide how to resolve it. Petrie and I only need to question Delaney.'

'I suppose that's some consolation.'

She put down her magazine. It lay open on the table at a page showing a photograph of Jean Harlow, encased in ivory satin elegance. She was holding out one side of her dress's sunray-pleated skirt so that the photographer's artful lighting dissolved the fabric into a luminous shimmer. The photograph was a sad reminder to de Silva that his camera still lay unused.

'Shanti?' Jane frowned. 'I said did you mention Betty Falconer's information to Petrie? Surely, it's relevant now?'

He rallied, 'It certainly is, and I did, but he asked me to keep quiet about it for the moment.'

'Probably wise until you've had a chance to talk to Delaney. Did you speak to Mrs de Vere about Charles Pashley?'

'Yes. She made it very clear she disliked him – there seems to have been a lot of professional animosity between them – but that alone isn't proof that she killed him. Like all the others, she was able to account for her movements that evening up until she retired for the night. After that, we're back to relying on Chung's honesty.'

He yawned. 'I feel as if it's been a long day already. What have you been doing while I've been away?'

'Oh, I went to the Sunday service.'

Ruefully, he realised that in the absence of church bells, he had forgotten it was a Sunday. He sighed. 'I'm sorry I didn't keep you company. If this trip hadn't turned into such a bus driver's holiday, I would have.'

'Busman's holiday, dear. Afterwards I went to a very interesting talk about dolphins and whales given by a professor of marine biology who happens to be on board, then I came back here.'

'I'm glad you enjoyed it.'

There was a knock at the door. 'Come in!' called de Silva.

'Message from the captain, sir,' said the steward who entered.

De Silva groaned inwardly. What now? He slit open the envelope. 'It's about Harry Delaney,' he said with a frown. 'He was due to perform at a morning concert and didn't turn up. He's not in his cabin, and it seems that no one's seen him since yesterday.'

CHAPTER 15

'Any news of Delaney yet?' asked Petrie. He had summoned de Silva to the smoking room in Cabin Class. It was quiet there in the middle of the afternoon.

'Not yet, sir. But Captain McDowell has lent me the services of a few of the crew to help in the search. It can't be long.'

'I hope not. I can't imagine why he'd suffer the same fate as Pashley, but it would be reassuring to find him.'

'Indeed, sir.'

De Silva's stomach rumbled. He'd eaten nothing since breakfast except a few of the sandwiches Jane had ordered from room service. He thought wistfully of the lavish lunch buffet usually set out in the Tourist Class dining room. He hoped he wasn't going to have to miss dinner too.

William Petrie got up from the wing-backed armchair in which he was sitting. 'I can't see what more we can do. The crew probably know this ship like the backs of their hands. Best to let them get on with it. Something did occur to me though. If Venetia de Vere isn't trying to pull the wool over our eyes about this ring of hers, we ought to question that steward again. He has a pass key to all the cabins and could easily slip in when the occupants are out. What's his name?'

'Chung, sir.'

'Right; we'll deal with him straight away. I suppose the

111

same point applies to the other stewards who've been on duty for the corridor, but they'll have to wait. After we've seen Chung, we should go to dinner. I expect Mrs de Silva is becoming as tired as is Lady Caroline of this wretched business impinging on our respective holidays.'

* * *

In Captain McDowell's not entirely successful attempt to keep Charles Pashley's murder quiet, Chung had been removed from duty in Cabin Class and put to work in the kitchens. As Petrie and de Silva approached them, the heat intensified. De Silva felt sweat trickle down his back under his shirt and bead his forehead. His hands were clammy. He felt sorry for Chung if the man had done nothing worse than have an occasional doze when he was on duty. It was hard to be forced to exchange an easy job in Cabin Class for such unpleasant conditions.

William Petrie must be fitter than he was. He seemed far less troubled by the oppressive heat. De Silva hoped the excursion was going to be worthwhile. For the moment, he was sceptical. Why would Chung want the ring? They were a long way from land. Had he taken it with a view to selling it in a bazaar, he was going to have a long wait, and during that time, he might be found out. More likely that, if he had stolen it, it would have been on someone's orders. But whose?

Steam and strong aromas of baking, roasting, and frying wafted towards them. The air was full of bellowed orders: a jangle of Chinese, Malay, Tamil, Sinhalese and English. The young officer who had been their guide ushered them into a small, stuffy room furnished with a table and two hard chairs.

'If you'd be so kind as to take a seat and wait here, gentlemen, I'll fetch the man you want.'

Chung wore a sweat-stained vest and a pair of loose white cotton trousers rolled up above his knees. His bare arms and calves glistened. He crooked an arm and dragged the inside of the elbow across his perspiring face.

'You wanted to speak to me, sirs?' he asked, shifting his weight from one foot to the other.

'What do you know about a ring that was stolen from Mrs de Vere's cabin?' William Petrie asked sternly.

Chung's eyes widened. 'Nothing, sir. I swear it.'

'Are you sure you never used your pass key to enter the cabin?'

'Of course not, sir, and I would never steal.' A desperate note quavered in Chung's voice.

'If you're lying, you know you'll lose your job.'

'Yes, sir.' The words came out in a whisper. 'But it's the truth, sir.'

'At any time, did you see anyone go to the cabins who had no business to be there?'

Chung looked miserable, and de Silva felt a stab of pity. On occasion, he had experienced the rough side of Archie Clutterbuck's tongue. For a half-educated man of Chung's lowly status, Petrie's questioning must feel a thousand times worse.

'No, sir.'

'Have you ever noticed anything suspicious? For example, passengers leaving their cabins after they've apparently retired for the night? It will go very hard with you if there's something you don't tell us.'

'I understand, sir.' Chung hesitated.

The air was thick with silence, finally broken by Petrie. 'I think there is something. Out with it, man.'

'Sometimes, after she has returned from dinner, Mrs de Vere goes out again late at night.'

'Did she do that on the night Mr Pashley was killed?' asked de Silva.

Chung thought for a moment. 'Yes, sir, but she came back very quickly, and she looked angry.'

'Why didn't you tell us this before?' asked Petrie.

Staring at his feet, Chung mumbled something inaudible. Petrie scowled and leant back in his chair. 'No doubt she made it worth your while to keep her comings and goings to yourself. Very well, you may get back to your duties. Don't forget my warning.'

* * *

'It's a relief to spend a normal evening,' said Jane. 'I'm glad William Petrie decided we all should.'

They sat in the Tourist Class bar, waiting for the second sitting for dinner to be announced. De Silva swirled the whisky in his glass and ice cubes chinked against crystal. He wished he could relax but it wasn't easy.

'I don't see anyone we know,' Jane remarked, surveying the room. 'I thought the Rosses might be here, but then I haven't come across them all day. I do hope neither of them are unwell.'

'If she's lost again, that can be the next job for the crew.'

Jane smiled. 'I'm glad you haven't lost your sense of humour.'

'I feel my grasp on it is tenuous to say the least,' he said with a sigh.

The ship's announcements system crackled into life to tell them dinner was served. Fortunately, there were several Indian dishes on the menu, and an assortment of tasty vegetable samosas and fiery curries went a long way to improving de Silva's spirits. After they'd drunk their coffee, served in dainty, gilt-rimmed cups decorated with the insignia of the Blue Star line, they decided to take a walk before turning in. On the way, they went to their cabin for de Silva to fetch his camera. With so much going on, he must remember to make the effort to use it, and he'd been wanting to try some night shots.

It was quiet on deck but not silent, even though the night time sounds were different from those at home at Sunnybank. The murmur of water as the ship cut through the waves, and the low throb of the engines replaced the familiar hum of insects and rustle of nocturnal creatures. Instead of the dark shapes of trees and bushes to guide his way, he gazed out over an endless expanse of liquorice water, where moonlight gleamed on the frothy white crests of the waves. He tried a few shots, hoping the Kodak was up to capturing the beauty of the contrast of light and shade, but eventually, not wanting to waste too much film if it wasn't, he tucked it back in its case, content simply to look.

The Arabian Sea: and to the south, the Indian Ocean. His own island, the teardrop of India, was there too. Then water, broken only by a few specks of land, until you reached the Southern Ocean and the frozen wastes of Antarctica. Feeling suddenly very small, he put an arm around Jane's shoulders. 'Are you feeling cold yet?'

She snuggled up to him. 'Let's stay a bit longer. It's so beautiful out here.'

'I wonder how things are at home.'

She smiled. 'I'm sure Prasanna and Nadar are getting along fine without you.'

'Not too well, I hope. And my dahlias. The shoots are still very tender. Snails are bound to eat them if Anif isn't watchful.'

'I expect he will be. Anif's a good worker. I'm sure he's taking great care of your beloved car too.'

He smiled. 'Funny to think that if we'd chosen a later passage, we'd never have heard of Charles Pashley. We might have spent the time relaxing and enjoying ourselves.'

'It would have been nice, but never mind.'

They gazed at the view and chatted, until Jane shivered and wrapped her cashmere shawl tighter around herself. 'I'm starting to feel a little chilly now. It must be past midnight. Shall we go in?'

As they turned away from the rail, a door banged, and they saw that a woman had come out on deck. She started to pace up and down, her arms clasped across her chest and her head bowed, as if she was deeply distressed. Jane strained her eyes to see in the dim light.

'That's Barbara Ross,' she whispered with a puzzled frown. 'I wonder what she's doing out here by herself at this hour? She looks very upset. Should we go over to her? Or do you think she'd rather be left alone?'

De Silva shrugged. 'I'm no expert in these matters, my love. I leave that to you.'

Barbara Ross had stopped by a door some way off from the one through which she had come out on deck.

'Oh dear,' Jane whispered again. 'I don't know where that door leads. What if she gets lost again? We may have to follow her after all.'

Opening the door, Barbara Ross walked through it. Jane went to follow her, then there was a scream. Barbara Ross emerged and stumbled to the rail. Afraid she might come to harm, de Silva hurried over to her. As he caught her arm, she turned a stricken face towards him before crumpling to the deck in a dead faint.

Jane was by his side. 'I'll stay with her. You go and find help.'

Inside, de Silva collided with a steward coming from the direction of the Tourist Class bar. He sent the man to fetch Doctor Brady, then returned to the deck.

Standing on the threshold of the small space Barbara Ross had so hastily left, he noticed a sickly, metallic smell. When his eyes became accustomed to the darkness inside, he made out that what she had found was a storeroom with lifejackets and wooden boxes stacked against the walls. But it was the other thing that the storeroom contained that made his heartbeat quicken.

Lying on his back in a pool of his own blood, was Harry Delaney; the dress shirt that should have been white was crimson. His eyes were open, and his mouth gaped. De Silva went in and crouched beside him. Automatically, he felt for a pulse, although he was already sure there was no possibility of the singer still being alive. Delaney's skin was clammy and cold.

A voice behind him made him start. Looking round, he saw a young officer. His face was pale. 'Is he dead, sir?'

'I'm afraid so. There's nothing we can do for him, but the lady who found him needs help. I've already sent a steward for Doctor Brady, and I'd like you to notify Captain McDowell and Mr William Petrie.'

'Right away, sir.'

The young officer hurried off, and de Silva stood up. He saw that Barbara Ross had regained consciousness, and Jane had helped her to a chair. He went over to them.

'Is it Delaney?' asked Jane.

'Yes; dead, I'm afraid. Stabbed in the neck.'

'Oh, how dreadful.'

'I've sent for Doctor Brady, and that young officer's gone to notify Petrie.'

Jane took off her cashmere shawl and wrapped it around Barbara Ross's shoulders. She was shivering violently, but de Silva saw beads of sweat on her forehead.

'The doctor's coming,' Jane said soothingly. 'And we'll get you something hot to drink.'

'All that blood… I wasn't expecting…' Barbara Ross clapped a hand over her mouth. 'I'm going to be sick!'

Quickly, Jane helped her to the rail.

By the time the nausea had passed, Doctor Brady arrived. He carried his black bag and wore jacket and trousers, but a glimpse of striped pyjamas showed at the end of the jacket sleeves. With Jane's help, he walked Barbara Ross back to her chair, then crouched down beside her for a few moments, talking to her quietly.

'My nurse will be here soon,' he said when he stood up. 'She'll take Mrs Ross to lie down in the infirmary until she's fully recovered. Would you be so kind as to stay with her until then, Mrs de Silva?'

Jane nodded.

Brady went over to Delaney's body and studied it. 'Who's this, de Silva?'

'Harry Delaney. He was a singer with the entertainment crew.'

'Ah, I heard something about one of the crew going missing, but I didn't pay much attention. So, this is him, eh?'

'Yes.'

He bent down for a closer look at the body then straightened up. 'If you've no objection, I'll make arrangements for it to be removed immediately. I'm sure the captain won't want passengers alarmed. Is he aware of what's happened?'

'I've sent someone to inform him, and William Petrie too.'

'Good. Lucky there's room for another body in our little improvised mortuary.' He beckoned to the young officer. 'Get a stretcher from the infirmary and find someone to help you carry the body. We'd better get on with it.'

* * *

'What do you think about the time of death, Brady?' asked Petrie.

'At least twelve hours ago. When was he reported missing?'

'Yesterday.'

118

'Then it may be longer. What's the place where he was found used for?'

'Storing emergency flares, and spare lifejackets for anyone who wouldn't have time to return to their cabins in the event of an emergency,' said de Silva.

Petrie looked down at the marble slab where Delaney lay. 'When did anyone last go in there?'

'Regrettably, not during the search. The chief purser admitted it was treated as a low priority because of what it was used for.'

The contents of Delaney's pockets lay on a shelf nearby: a wallet, some loose change, a handkerchief, his crew pass, a ring, and a small pouch of white powder. De Silva sniffed the powder. Chemical with a trace of sweetness. He recognised it from his Colombo days.

'What is it?' asked Petrie.

'Cocaine.'

'So, our Mr Delaney had his vices.'

'It appears so.'

Petrie picked up the ring and turned it round, studying it. It was engraved with two interlaced Vs.

'I think we'll take this with us and show it to Mrs de Vere,' he said.

There was a knock at the door and the nurse de Silva had seen before came in.

'How's Mrs Ross?' asked Petrie.

'She's better now, sir.'

'I instructed Nurse Forbes here to give the lady something to calm her,' said Brady. 'Not surprising she was upset. Not many women, or men for that matter, would behave with equanimity in such circumstances.'

'Has her husband been informed?'

Brady looked at Nurse Forbes.

'Yes, Doctor Brady. He's coming shortly. He had to be woken up.'

'Hm,' said the doctor. 'He must be a sound sleeper if he didn't notice his wife had gone.'

* * *

Barbara Ross's face was red and blotchy from crying. 'I'm sorry,' she said shakily. 'I'm being such a baby. That poor man. It's just it was so horrible, and I wasn't expecting it.'

'There's no need to apologise, my dear,' said Jane. 'You've had a very nasty shock.'

Barbara Ross tried to sit up but fell back on the pillow again. 'Oh dear, I feel rather woozy.'

'If you don't mind my asking, why were you wandering around the ship on your own so late in the evening?'

'I feel so stupid. James and I had a silly argument earlier on. I'm afraid he gets very bell… bell…' She hiccoughed and started to cry again.

'Belligerent?'

'Yes. When he's had too much to drink, you know? I should never have let it spoil the lovely time we've been having, but after he went to sleep, I couldn't settle. I thought a walk around the deck might help, so I dressed and went out. But then I got in a muddle and lost my way.'

A look of alarm came over her face. 'Have they told James where I am?'

'Yes. I'm sure he'll be here soon.'

Barbara Ross hid her face in her hands. 'He'll be furious with me,' she said miserably.

'Everything's been explained to him. I think it's more likely he'll be relieved that you're unharmed.'

There were voices outside. Barbara Ross stiffened. 'That's him now.'

Accompanied by Doctor Brady, James Ross came into the room.

'Your wife has had a very unpleasant experience,' Brady was saying. 'I've prescribed rest for a day or two. You might both prefer to keep to your cabin. I fear there may be rumours after this. With the shock she's had, I don't recommend exposing her to the distress of facing the curiosity of other passengers.'

He stood aside, and Ross came forward to put his arms around his wife. She rested her head against his shoulder. 'I'm sorry,' Jane heard him mutter.

She saw Doctor Brady smile in her direction and nodded. 'We'll leave the two of you in peace,' she said.

CHAPTER 16

Captain McDowell's eyebrows almost met in the middle. With his first officer in charge on the bridge, he had hoped for a peaceful night. 'It's imperative this is hushed up,' he growled. 'The owners will be furious if there's more damage done to their ship's reputation. One murder on board's serious enough, but two…'

De Silva buried the thought that the last thing the murderer, or murderers, were likely to have been concerned about were the profits of the owners of the Blue Star Line. Instead, he adopted a solemn expression and did his best to help William Petrie reassure his old shipmate that every effort would be made to conduct the investigation discreetly.

'Not an easy task, I admit,' said McDowell, calming a little.

'Who would be able to tell us more about Delaney?' asked Petrie.

McDowell shrugged. 'I've had no dealings with him. The best man to speak to will be the chief purser. He's in overall charge of the entertainment side. He may be able to direct you to other members of the crew it would be worth your while talking to.'

'Thank you. We'll leave you to your well-deserved night's rest.'

'Keep me informed of developments, won't you?'

'Of course.'

'Oh, and by the way, I've decided to hold Pashley's body on the ship until we reach Port Said. You can tell Brady the same goes for Delaney.'

* * *

'Poor chap,' remarked Petrie as they left McDowell's cabin. 'It's hardly his fault that there've been two murders on board. But although you and I see that, the owners may take a different view if their profits are adversely affected. The sooner we get to the bottom of this, the better. What do you suggest?'

De Silva pondered. 'I think we should sleep on it, sir,' he said after a few moments. 'Questioning any of the crew or the passengers so late at night's bound to cause comment. If it's not been done yet, I'll ensure that the storeroom's secured from prying eyes.'

Petrie looked at his wristwatch. 'You're right. It's nearly three o'clock in the morning. When you're done, get some sleep. We'll meet in my cabin later.'

* * *

'Oh Shanti, you look worn out.'

When he returned from making sure that the storeroom door was shut and padlocked, he found Jane in their cabin.

'I am tired, but you must be too.'

He sank into an armchair, stretched his legs as far as they would go and let his eyes close.

'Your shoes have blood on them, dear,' said Jane. 'Take them off and I'll wipe them for you.'

'I'm not surprised. That storeroom was very small, and it was all over the floor. If the murderer was expecting that, I imagine they took the precaution of wearing top clothes they could dispose of over the side along with the murder weapon.'

'Will you do anything more tonight?'

He shook his head. 'Captain McDowell made it very clear he doesn't want this to get out. That will be difficult, of course, but if we start our investigations late at night, we may as well turn on the loudspeaker system and make a public announcement. Fortunately, we still have many miles of sea on our side. If anyone wants to leave the ship before Suez and Port Said, they'll have to be very good at swimming.'

'Do you think Mrs de Vere did it? Should you question her again? And what about Betty Falconer? She might have more to tell us.'

De Silva yawned. 'It all needs thinking about, but I doubt Venetia de Vere would have stabbed Delaney. Petrie and I saw her on deck one day making a tremendous fuss about a bit of blood when a steward cut his hand.'

'That does make it seem unlikely she's the murderer. Who else might have wanted Delaney dead?'

He shrugged. 'I don't know, and my head's as heavy as an elephant. Time for bed. There'll be a lot to do later.'

CHAPTER 17

In the way he wished it would more often, sleep ironed out the creases in de Silva's brain. When he woke, he knew what he must do next.

An enquiry about the man who had filled the steward, Chung's, post brought an assurance from the chief purser that he was reliable.

'He's worked on this ship for many years, Inspector. Never put a foot wrong. He's elderly, so tends to be given lighter duties, and ones he can perform during the daytime, but we needed someone who was absolutely trustworthy.'

De Silva thought, but refrained from remarking, that all the crew ought to be trustworthy. 'Where is he now?'

'He may be resting after his night shift.'

'All the same, I'd like to speak to him. Would you fetch him, please?'

The elderly Malay who stood before him a little while later exuded an air of unruffled composure. Under his white turban, his gentle brown eyes gazed out at the world calmly. De Silva had the impression that Ahmad wasn't a man who was interested in idle gossip.

As de Silva asked him about the comings and goings of the passengers on his corridor on the nights since Charles Pashley's death, he listened attentively and didn't answer for several moments. When at last he spoke, it was in a deep, rumbling voice. If the information he gave was correct, and de Silva was impressed with his powers of recall, nothing out of the ordinary had occurred. Once the passengers had returned from dinner, none of them had gone out again. In fact, Venetia de Vere had taken many of her meals in her cabin and yesterday hadn't left it at all.

What conclusion was to be drawn from that? Thanking Ahmad for his help and sending him back to his rest, de Silva pondered this development. If Venetia de Vere hadn't left her cabin, she couldn't have gone to meet Harry Delaney in that storeroom, so who had? It didn't remove the need to confront her, but for now, there was the pianist, Betty Falconer, to be questioned.

* * *

Betty Falconer was an attractive woman in her late thirties. She was clearly unnerved by the summons to the chief purser's office, and de Silva resolved to do his best to put her at her ease.

'No one is accusing you of anything,' he said gently. 'But we believe you may have information that is important to an investigation we're conducting.'

The chief purser interrupted. 'It's a confidential matter, Miss Falconer. I trust we can rely on you not to repeat this conversation.'

'Of course.'

'You mentioned to a lady on board that the singer, Harry Delaney, was complaining of a passenger who was becoming an embarrassment to him. I'm sure I don't need to remind you that everyone working on the ship is banned from fraternising with our guests in private—'

Betty Falconer flushed. 'I'm not sure I should say... I might be wrong.'

'I was going on to say, but on this occasion, I can promise you that nothing you tell me will go any further.'

She looked relieved. 'Thank you. I wouldn't want to get him into any trouble.'

'Who is it, Miss Falconer?' asked de Silva.

'Must he find out it was me who told you?'

He gave her a kindly smile. 'That won't be necessary.'

She hesitated. 'A lady called Venetia de Vere. At first, he boasted about how one of the wealthy passengers was besotted with him. He said it started not long after we left Hong Kong. After a while, it wasn't hard to guess who he meant. I often play for the tea dances, and when Mrs de Vere attended, she always made a great fuss if he was already engaged to dance with someone else. When I teased him, he made a joke of it. Laughed about the presents she gave him and the money. He said it was pathetic the way she tried to buy his affection.'

What a charmer, thought de Silva. 'Did he ever mention comments she made about any of the other passengers?'

'I'm not sure. Oh yes, there was one. He said she complained a lot about one of the passengers whose cabin was near hers.'

'Was the name Charles Pashley?'

She considered the question for a few moments then shook her neatly coiffured head. 'I can't say for certain. It might have been.' She looked puzzled. 'Why are you asking me these questions? Has something happened to Harry?'

'I'm afraid I can't divulge our reasons but thank you for your help.'

As the chief purser showed Betty Falconer out, de Silva reflected that it wasn't going to be easy to keep this second murder a secret for long either.

'I hope you learnt what you wanted, Inspector,' the chief purser said when he'd closed the door. 'A bad business this. Never known anything like it in all the years I've worked for the Blue Star Line.'

'How many years would that be?'

'Eighteen. Ever since the end of the war, and always on the *Jewel*.'

'I suppose you've sailed the route from Hong Kong to England many times.'

'Dozens.'

A thought occurred to de Silva. It might not be important, but he liked to be clear on the facts.

'Apart from the passengers who joined the ship at Colombo, did the rest come on board at Hong Kong?'

'Most of them, but there were a few who joined us later.'

'Can you give me the names?'

'They'll be on the passenger list.'

'I'd be grateful if you'd check it and let me know.'

'Very well, Inspector.'

CHAPTER 18

The following morning, a message arrived from Scotland Yard in London.

'It doesn't tell us much,' said Petrie as they were on their way to see Venetia de Vere. 'As I expected, there's nothing untoward about Clara Pilkington or Venetia de Vere and no information about Mrs Meadows that might throw suspicion on her. Official records also confirm that Arthur Chiltern left England for Hong Kong five years ago, and George Ryder was sent out as a missionary to China in 1926. Nothing on Diana March, which accords with her story that this will be her first visit to England.'

At the door to Venetia de Vere's cabin, they exchanged glances. They had agreed that Petrie would be the one to break the news, and de Silva would observe the novelist's reactions. 'Ready?' asked Petrie in a low tone. His expression was grim.

'Yes, sir.'

'Then let's get on with it.' He raised his hand and knocked. A woman's voice called out for them to come in.

The effect the stateroom had on de Silva was less powerful the second time around. Its occupant was also looking less glamorous than she had on their previous visit: her hair not as immaculate and her eyes sad in her heavily made-up face. The practised smile came wanly to her lips.

'Won't you sit down, gentlemen? I can't imagine what

use I can be to you, but I assume you have more questions for me about Charles Pashley's death.'

'Not about Mr Pashley's death, Mrs de Vere.' Petrie took the chair she indicated. 'I'm afraid there has been another unpleasant occurrence on board.'

De Silva watched her face intently. Did it show any alarm? He thought not. The impression he still had was that something had made her deeply despondent.

'I've been unwell since yesterday, Mr Petrie and not left my cabin. As I said, I can't imagine how I can be of any use to you, but please continue.'

She gave a brittle laugh. 'My critics, the late Charles Pashley among them, have sometimes accused me of having an over-active imagination. I'll do my best to put it at your service.'

'Thank you,' said Petrie gravely. 'I fear, however, that this is no laughing matter. I'm sorry to say there's been another murder.'

De Silva saw Venetia de Vere's hand tighten on the arm of her chair. There was a perceptible tremor in her voice.

'Who?'

'A man called Harry Delaney. One of the ship's—'

Venetia de Vere's stifled scream stopped Petrie going any further. Her face crumpled, and she seemed to struggle to breathe. Petrie shot de Silva a meaningful look.

'Are you unwell, Mrs de Vere? Shall we call your maid?'

She shook her head; tears welled and spilled down her powdered cheeks, leaving dark runnels. A bout of shivering seized her. She certainly gave the impression that this was the first time she'd heard of Delaney's death. Either she was an accomplished actress, or she was innocent, thought de Silva.

'Are you sure you wouldn't like us to call your maid?' asked Petrie again. 'Or Doctor Brady?'

She drew a deep breath and the shivering subsided. 'No, that won't be necessary.'

'Forgive me,' resumed Petrie. 'I hadn't expected the news to cause you such distress, but I must ask you some questions.'

She produced a lace handkerchief and dried her eyes. 'Very well.'

'What was your connection to Harry Delaney?'

'I had none.'

Petrie reached into his pocket and brought out the ring with the initials VV. 'I believe this is your ring. Can you explain why we found it in his possession?'

She stared at the ring with dismay. Bowing her head, it was a long time before she spoke, then she looked up. 'I suppose it's useless to try to hide it anymore. There was something between us. I was in love with him, and I thought he loved me. But it turned out that I was wrong. As for the ring, I'm sorry, but after he broke with me, I said it was stolen because I wanted him accused of theft if he was found with it.'

She started to cry again. From the expression on William Petrie's face, de Silva guessed that an emotional situation such as this was one that put the Englishman at a disadvantage. He was probably wishing he was anywhere but in this cabin. A feeling, de Silva had to admit, that to some extent he shared.

The lace handkerchief lay in Mrs de Vere's lap, a soggy mess. He pulled his own from his pocket, relived to see it was a clean one, and handed it to her.

'Thank you, Inspector,' she said shakily. She gave him a wan smile. 'They say there's no fool like an old fool.' She was silent for a moment then asked how Delaney had died.

'He was stabbed, ma'am. But we think his death would have been quick. He wouldn't have suffered,' he added.

'It's kind of you to try to comfort me, Inspector. Have you found out who's responsible?'

'Not yet, but if you know anything that might help us to find them, please tell us.'

She spread her hands in a gesture of hopelessness. 'I'm sorry, Inspector. I realise now how little I knew him.'

* * *

'Poor lady,' said Jane. 'What a dreadful shock she must have had.'

After their interview with Venetia de Vere, Petrie and de Silva had parted company to return to their wives.

He swallowed some of the tea a steward had brought to their cabin at Jane's request. It was hot and fragrant: a reminder of home. As this case became ever more puzzling, it was tempting to wish they had stayed in Nuala. So far, the cruise hadn't borne much resemblance to a holiday.

'Shanti?'

He brought his attention back to what Jane was saying.

'I said, did you believe Mrs de Vere?'

'Her distress seemed genuine, and to add to it, the old fellow who's taken Chung's place at the end of that corridor confirms that she didn't leave her cabin around the time of Delaney's death. Also, she has a horror of blood.' He explained abut Venetia de Vere's fuss over the steward's cut hand.

'I can see that would make it unlikely she could stab Delaney,' said Jane. 'Even without the fact she didn't leave her cabin.'

He drained his tea and put down the cup. 'That was very good.'

'Have another. It will help you to think.'

She touched her fingertips to the outside of the silver teapot. 'It's still nice and hot. Are you feeling hungry?'

'I will be soon, but I'd rather order lunch here if you don't mind. I need time to think.'

Jane lifted the pot and poured more tea into his cup.

Aromatic steam drifted towards his nostrils. He smiled. 'Tea: the British panacea for all problems. Perhaps we'll find the answer in the leaves, like a teller of fortunes. That would make my life very much easier.'

'What are you going to do if the crimes haven't been solved before we arrive in Port Said?'

'Goodness knows. I hope it won't come to that.'

'By the way.' She stood up, went to the little bureau in one corner of the cabin and picked up a sheet of paper. 'The chief purser sent the information you asked for about passengers who joined the ship after it left Hong Kong.'

De Silva took the sheet and ran his eye down the list. A few passengers had joined the ship at Singapore and more at Calcutta. One of those was Charles Pashley.

CHAPTER 19

'So,' said William Petrie gravely, putting down the list. 'We have three possibilities: firstly, whoever killed Pashley joined the ship at Calcutta when *he* did; secondly, they came on board earlier, knowing that he would be travelling from Calcutta, or thirdly, his presence came as a nasty surprise to them.'

He sighed. 'It's useful to establish facts, de Silva, but with that number of possibilities, I'm damned if I see how it advances the case. All the occupants of the other cabins on the corridor have been on board since Hong Kong. The only thing this piece of information proves is that it could have been any one of them.'

They were in the smoking room. Once again, it was quiet. Glumly, de Silva took back the list. Petrie was right. Still, the information might turn out to be relevant in some way.

Petrie ran a hand through his hair, a gesture that made him look almost boyish, except de Silva noticed that the lines around his eyes had deepened during the voyage. He was reminded that he wasn't the only person whose holiday had been disrupted. Petrie had probably been looking forward to a respite from duty too.

'What have we got then, de Silva? Now the steward, Chung, has changed his story about Mrs de Vere, we know we can't necessarily trust his word, and we may not be able to rely on his vigilance either. I appreciate that what he told you about the times the passengers retired for the night accords with what they've said, but have you checked their accounts independently?'

'I was concerned that questioning more people would cause suspicion, sir, but as the passengers claimed they were in public places, the stewards should be able to confirm their stories for us. Cabin Class is far less busy than Tourist Class. The only exception is Canon Ryder who said he was alone in the chapel for a while before retiring to bed.'

Petrie shrugged. 'He seems an unlikely suspect in any case.' He paused to light a cigarette then held out the gold case to de Silva. 'Change your mind? I find tobacco helps the thought processes.'

Tempted, de Silva took one. His thought processes could certainly do with some help just now.

'Thank you, sir.'

'My tobacconist in London blends these for me. He ships all over the world.'

De Silva took a puff; the tobacco was rich and soothing. 'It's excellent, thank you.'

'By the way, has Pashley's key turned up yet?'

'Not to my knowledge.'

Scratching his head, Petrie frowned. 'We only have Chung's word that Pashley lost it and needed to be let into his cabin. No one else was present at the time. What if Chung's lying about it? If Pashley was incapacitated, Chung might have relieved him of the key unnoticed, then given it to the murderer so they could enter Pashley's cabin later. In any case, making out that Pashley's key had been stolen would deflect awkward questions about how unauthorised entry to the cabin was gained, the obvious alternative being with Chung's pass key. If he's right up to his neck in this sordid business, it's also plausible he carried out the crime on someone else's orders. As nothing was stolen, I doubt it was on his own behalf.'

But if Chung hadn't stolen the key, thought de Silva, it was still possible there was a different third party involved. One who could have obtained the key from Pashley, probably after spiking his drink. If this third party was the killer, or gave the key to a guilty passenger, Chung would have had to turn a blind eye to their going to Pashley's cabin. That was entirely plausible – they were already aware that Chung couldn't be trusted.

If only they knew who Pashley had been drinking with that evening. Suddenly, he remembered the remark of the bar steward in the Tourist Class bar. He'd said Pashley had been talking with one of the crew on the eve of the night he was killed. De Silva had let the information pass, assuming Pashley had been after gossip for one of his newspaper columns. But what if he'd been wrong and missed a crucial clue? It occurred to him that if there was a connection between Pashley's and Delaney's murder, they might find answers there.

William Petrie nodded when he voiced the idea. 'I agree. I believe Captain McDowell's already given orders that Delaney's cabin is to be left untouched and locked until he says otherwise. That should give us time to look through Delaney's effects.'

Petrie stretched out his long legs and eased his shoulders. Once more, de Silva noticed signs of fatigue on his face.

'We still have unanswered questions about who had the opportunity to kill our two victims,' went on Petrie. 'Let's turn to the motive, starting with Mrs Pilkington. By her own account, Pashley was a casual acquaintance. She's wealthy, and according to the information we have, not a whiff of scandal has ever been attached to her. Unless there's some skeleton buried deep in her closet that Pashley threatened to expose, where's her motive?'

'No obvious one, sir, I agree.'

'As for Delaney's murder, we have no reason to believe

she was even aware of his presence. The same goes for Mrs March and her fiancé. Chung hasn't changed his story that they returned to their staterooms at two o'clock on the night of Pashley's murder and didn't leave them again. I'm reasonably confident he's telling the truth there.'

'Why's that, sir?' ventured de Silva.

'Can you really imagine a woman like Diana March committing such violent crimes? And Chiltern is wealthy and privileged. What would be in it for him?'

De Silva wasn't convinced that a woman wouldn't commit a violent crime but decided to hold his peace for the moment.

'We know Venetia de Vere's dislike of Charles Pashley was vehement. We also know about her unfortunate affair with Delaney.'

'But don't you remember, sir? She told us she didn't leave her cabin because she was unwell. The new steward on duty, Ahmad, confirmed it, so she had no opportunity to meet Delaney and stab him.'

'You're right. But it's not entirely conclusive. She could have killed Charles Pashley or paid someone to kill either man for her. That leaves Canon Ryder. I suppose we can't discount him yet, but I'd be very surprised if he had anything to do with either death. Oh, and Mrs Meadows, Clara Pilkington's unfortunate companion. As I mentioned once before, I think she should be questioned without her employer present. This fellow Ahmad seems observant. Find out from him if there's a regular time when Meadows is off-duty in her cabin. You can approach her then.'

He glanced at his watch. 'I promised to meet a friend who's on board. Keep up some semblance of normality. But for how much longer we'll be able to, I wouldn't like to say. We'll speak later, de Silva. Put your thinking cap on. I'm relying on you.'

* * *

'You may be right that he means it as a compliment,' said de Silva to Jane 'But it's one I don't deserve.'

'Of course, you do. Your record of solving cases is excellent.'

'This might be the one that shatters it.' He groaned. 'I suppose I should go and speak to old Ahmad about Mrs Meadows. With a bit of luck, there'll be a time when she's alone today. What are you planning to do?'

'Lady Caroline's asked me to join her for a stroll on the Promenade Deck and tea in the Cabin Class lounge.'

He smiled. 'Very nice. I'm glad the two of you get on well.'

'We do seem to. We share the same taste in reading, and I think she enjoys having someone to talk to about England, as I do.'

'I wouldn't have put Lady Caroline down as a reader of detective novels.'

'What would you expect her to read?'

'Something more ladylike.'

'Such as?'

'Elegantly written literary novels perhaps. Ouch!' He doubled up as the cushion landed squarely in his stomach. 'What was that for?'

'Making such a condescending assumption. She's a very modern woman.'

He chuckled. 'Sorry.' He hauled himself out of his chair and dropped the cushion onto the seat behind him. 'I must be off. Enjoy your tea.'

In the little room at the mouth of the corridor that de Silva was beginning to know far too well, Ahmad sat in quiet contemplation. De Silva felt rather envious. He soon elicited the information that Mrs Meadows usually spent about two hours before dinner in her own cabin. Presumably

Mrs Pilkington liked to rest, and the services of her maid were enough when she was ready to dress.

De Silva looked at his watch. He had plenty of time. After a short debate with himself as to whether he should send a message in advance, he decided against it. It would backfire if Mrs Meadows mentioned the request to Mrs Pilkington, who was almost certain to interfere. He felt the need for some distraction: maybe he would fetch his camera and see if there were any interesting shots to take on deck.

When he returned to their cabin, Jane wasn't there; she must have already left to meet Lady Caroline.

He blinked as he emerged onto the Sun Deck. It brought it home to him that, for the last few days, he had been spending too much time indoors. Leaning over the starboard rail, he let the salty air fill his lungs. A sea breeze blew the smoke from the funnels to the port side of the ship, and the engines were too deep in its bowels for their oily smell to reach him. There was still no sign of land on the horizon, but there must be soon. They had reached the Gulf of Aden and would soon be in the Red Sea.

None of his attempts at framing interesting pictures of the view satisfied him. After a few minutes, he put his camera away. Perhaps Port Said would offer better pickings. He wondered if the city would be much different from Colombo. Would there be the same cacophony of hawkers shouting out the wares they had for sale; the same hooting of cars and trucks, nosing their way through crowds of people; the same jingle of rickshaw bells, and the same braying of pack donkeys? Would the smells be the same? Spices, incense, unwashed humanity, fish, and drains?

A small white dog trotted past at the end of a scarlet leash held by a smartly uniformed maid. The bow that held the little creature's silky hair back from its black button eyes was also scarlet. It reminded de Silva of Florence Clutterbuck's beloved pet, Angel.

At the thought of Nuala, de Silva fell to wondering how matters would have progressed if it had been Archie and Florence travelling with them rather than the Petries. The couples were very different: the Clutterbucks far closer to the conventional mould of the British abroad than the Petries.

He had to admit, William Petrie had turned out to be quite a surprise. He had taken the lead on most occasions; that was only to be expected, but he had also shown a willingness to treat a man who many of the British would have considered an inferior, as an equal. It was interesting how people often proved to be very different underneath the image suggested by the office they held. It was the same with uniforms. Frequently, they subsumed the individuality of the wearer: the vicar's clerical garb; the judge's wig and robes; his own policeman's uniform. To the casual observer, the people inside them were indistinguishable from each other.

He heard voices and saw that several groups of passengers had come out on deck. Consulting his watch once more, he realised that tea must be over. He had missed it, but for once, he was in no mood for cream cakes and scones.

CHAPTER 20

Mrs Meadows looked startled when she opened the cabin door to find de Silva there.

'Forgive me for coming unannounced, ma'am,' he said. 'If it won't inconvenience you, I'd be grateful for a few minutes of your time.'

She rallied. 'Certainly, Inspector. Please come in.'

Her cabin was like Charles Pashley's: a small sitting room, comfortably furnished, with a door leading off it that presumably led to the bedroom area. Mrs Meadows indicated an armchair. 'Do make yourself comfortable. I'm afraid I haven't any refreshments to offer you. If this is about Mr Pashley, I can't imagine how I can help you, but I'll do my best.'

'Did you have much to do with him?'

'As little as possible. I shared my employer's view of him. But of course, on a ship it's hard to ignore one's near neighbours. I exchanged a few civilities with him when it would have been rude not to do so.'

She smiled politely. De Silva looked for signs of tension in her expression or the way she held herself but found none.

'Have you been in Mrs Pilkington's employment for long?'

'I started working for her after my husband died suddenly five years ago. I needed to earn a living.' She paused.

'Oh, I can guess what you're thinking, Inspector. How do I put up with her? The answer is, she's kinder than you might suppose.'

'I'm glad to hear it.'

'She has her moods, but in her defence, she suffers terribly with an old injury to her hip. Doctor Brady often sends his nurse to give her massages in the hope of providing some relief, but I'm afraid it hasn't made much difference.'

Her voice caught in her throat and she coughed. 'Excuse me, I need a drink of water. I won't be a moment. There's a carafe in my bedroom.'

She left the room and de Silva heard the chink of a glass and the sound of water being poured.

While he waited, he looked around the room. A sewing basket was on the floor beside the chair where Mrs Meadows had been sitting. She seemed to be more interested in plain sewing than the delicate embroidery that Jane was fond of doing. The piece of work on top of the pile was a grey stocking. Where the wool had worn at the heel, the stocking was stretched over a wooden darning mushroom. A needle threaded with matching wool lay on top of it.

De Silva frowned. The colour of the wool reminded him of something he'd seen only recently. He delved into his memory and remembered. It was the scrap of grey wool he'd picked up on his sleeve in Charles Pashley's cabin.

Had he worn the same jacket that day? Thrusting both hands in his pockets, de Silva felt around. A handkerchief, some loose change, and something soft but stringy. A strand of wool. He pulled it out and held it against the stocking in the basket; it was an exact match.

His mind raced as he heard Mrs Meadows coming back. Had this mild little woman been in Pashley's cabin and if so, why? Was she involved in his murder? She was the last person he would have suspected, and he very much doubted she would have had the strength to carry out the crime alone. Yet now, he had to consider the serious possibility that she had played a part. If he was right, how was he going to catch her out?

'I'm terribly sorry, Inspector,' she said brightly as she returned to the room. 'This wretched cough. I've suffered with it since Calcutta. Probably an infection. Mrs Pilkington insisted I see Doctor Brady who's prescribed a linctus, but I'm afraid it doesn't seem to be helping a great deal. It becomes worse in the evenings. Thankfully, Mrs Pilkington doesn't require me to be on duty at dinner, so I may eat mine here in my cabin in peace.'

She raised the glass of water she carried to her lips and took a sip. De Silva noticed that a scrap of fuzz from the grey wool in the basket had also caught on the sleeve of her beige cardigan. He debated how to lay his trap.

'I hope you won't think me rude, Inspector,' Mrs Meadows resumed. 'But if there's nothing more I can help you with, I would like to rest.'

De Silva took a deep breath. He had better go in boldly. 'There is something.'

'Yes?'

'You told me that you had as little as possible to do with the late Mr Pashley.'

'That's correct.'

'In that case, can you explain what you were doing in his cabin shortly before his death?'

The look of alarm in Mrs Meadows' eyes told him that he had struck home.

'I… I wasn't in his cabin.'

He looked at her steadily. 'I believe you're lying, ma'am.'

The skin on her knuckles stretched over the bone; her cheeks flushed.

'No! I've told you. I avoided him as much as possible. Why would I want to visit him in his cabin?'

'That's what I'd like to know. We have evidence you were

147

there. If you're trying to protect someone, it's no use. We'll find out the truth in the end, so please answer my question.'

Gradually, the colour drained from Mrs Meadows' cheeks. A pulse beat in the hollow at the base of her throat. Like an egg that has received a too-sharp tap with the spoon, her face crumpled. She made for the door. She had almost grasped the handle when it opened. Framed in the half-lit space was Canon Ryder.

CHAPTER 21

He held out his arms and Mrs Meadows rushed into them. 'There, there, Angela,' he murmured. 'I'm here now. It's alright.'

She broke away. 'No, George, it's not alright. You don't understand.'

Looking over the top of her head, Ryder saw de Silva. Swiftly, his expression changed from one of surprise to calm. He stepped into the room and closed the door. 'Good afternoon, Inspector. Forgive me for intruding. I heard a commotion and was afraid that Mrs Meadows was in difficulties.'

De Silva was puzzled. If Ryder and Meadows had merely met as neighbours on the ship, it now appeared that they were more than that.

'Your concern does you credit, sir; perhaps you can help me too. I've reason to believe Mrs Meadows may be able to help with the inquiry into Charles Pashley's death. We were just discussing the events surrounding it. There's evidence that she went to Mr Pashley's cabin the day before he died. I've asked her to tell me the purpose of her visit.'

He paused, trying to read Ryder's expression, but it was unrevealing. The silence lengthened. 'As you and Mrs Meadows seem to be well acquainted, perhaps you can assist,' de Silva resumed. 'What did you mean by your remarks when you came in?'

He turned to Mrs Meadows. 'And you, ma'am; to what were you referring? What is it that Canon Ryder doesn't understand?'

Angela Meadows' lips clamped shut, and she stared at him stubbornly. Again, silence thickened the air like the approach of a monsoon storm.

At last, Ryder sighed. 'Very well, Inspector. You may as well know the truth. Mrs Meadows and I are brother and sister. She was trying to protect me.'

He reached behind him, and the door lock clicked. A chilly sensation started between de Silva's shoulder blades and crept up to the nape of his neck. He wasn't armed. What if Ryder was? He braced himself for a fight and hoped the cleric's reactions wouldn't be too quick for him. He seemed far too gentle to be a killer, but if de Silva had learnt one thing in his career, it was that you sometimes found the perpetrator of a crime in the most unlikely places. Had Ryder acted alone or was Mrs Meadows guilty too? He studied their faces, still finding it hard to believe that this seemingly harmless couple hid such a dark secret, but he was ready to fight if he had to.

The ghost of a smile came over Ryder's face. 'Have no fear, Inspector. My sister and I are not criminals. We both had good reasons for wanting Pashley gone – reasons I'll explain if you'll hear me out – but we weren't responsible for ridding the world of a viper who should have been destroyed long ago.'

The tension in de Silva's body eased a little, but he remained watchful. 'Go on,' he said. 'I'm listening.'

'I was an army chaplain during the war. Afterwards, I was sent by my bishop to work in a parish in an area of London called Soho. Its proximity to London's theatreland gives it a touch of glamour, but it's also notorious as a red-light district, and many of the streets are slums. It was a challenging task.'

He cleared his throat. 'Must we stand, Inspector? My sister looks very pale.'

Angela Meadows' chin lifted. 'You've no need to worry about me, George. I won't faint.'

'I'm sure you won't, but let's sit all the same.'

They sat down, de Silva in the room's only armchair, Ryder and his sister facing him on the sofa.

'Where to begin?' Ryder scratched his head. 'As I said, my bishop had set me a challenging task. I like to think I rose to it with some success in the time I was there. I particularly tried to help the young men and boys of the parish. Most of them lacked a good education and had dismal prospects. I set up a boxing club; arranged social events at the church hall – anything that might occupy them in a positive way and increase their self-confidence. I also hoped I might encourage them to look on me as a friend, so they would feel free to confide in me if they were in trouble.'

He stopped, and his sister reached for his hand. Her expression was haggard. 'You don't need to tell him any more, George. All he needs to know is that neither of us were involved in Pashley's murder.'

'I'm afraid that won't be enough, Angela,' Ryder said sadly. 'I've tried to excuse my actions by remembering the good I did in the parish, but I know how close I came to going astray.' A muscle worked in his cheek. 'I became too fond of one of my charges. He was sixteen and very impressionable.'

He paused, worrying at the patch of ragged skin on the edge of his thumb. 'We did nothing wrong,' he went on. 'I swear it. But rumours began to spread.'

The cleric looked so wretched that de Silva felt a twinge of pity. If Ryder was telling the truth, he was in the clear, but homosexuality was a sin in the eyes of the Church of England and a crime under British law. That applied throughout the Empire, and the penalty was life imprisonment. To de Silva, the punishment seemed harsh. The teachings of the Buddha were, at least on one interpretation, more compassionate. If love was coupled with loyalty and harmed no one, it was not necessarily forbidden.

'Rumours began to spread,' repeated Ryder. 'I'm convinced Charles Pashley was one of those who spread them. He lived close to where I was working. He was a writer – not a very successful one at that stage – supplementing his income with writing articles for local newspapers, and he already had a nose for scandal.'

'Do you think he recognised you here on the ship?'

'At first, I didn't think so. Back then, he hadn't taken much interest in the projects I set up, and many years have gone by. In any case, it's notable how one frequently disappears behind clerical black. Perhaps you find your uniform tends to have the same effect, Inspector?'

De Silva nodded.

'With these scars, my appearance had changed too.' He touched his face. 'But I'm afraid I was mistaken. A few days after we left Calcutta, we passed in the corridor. He greeted me and made it clear he hadn't forgotten.'

Angela Meadows jerked forward in her seat. Livid patches flared on her cheeks. 'Pashley was vicious. He may not have intended to expose George, but I'm sure he planned to glory in tormenting him with the fear that he might.'

Her brother reached for her hand. 'Try to be calm.'

'How can I be when I think of what that horrible man put us through? I wish I'd never gone to his cabin to plead with him to leave us alone. I should have known it would only feed his vanity.'

Putting her hand to his lips, Ryder kissed it. 'You acted from the best of motives, my dear.' He shrugged. 'I realised there was nothing to be done, except wait and pray that Pashley would keep my story to himself.'

Not entirely correct, thought de Silva. Murdering him would have provided the solution, but his gut instinct told him that Ryder was telling the truth.

'Going back to the boy,' said Ryder. 'He was terrified of being imprisoned and shunned me. For my part, I dreaded every ring of the telephone or knock at the door.'

His sister intervened. 'I told George he had to leave the country. Staying was too big a risk. My husband refused to discuss what was to be done. Even though George was blameless, he didn't want anything to do with him.'

'The rumours came to the bishop's ears,' Ryder went on. 'He offered me a way out. I could take up missionary work in China. I accepted, and in 1926, I left England. The work was hard, although rewarding, but as matters turned out, I had exchanged one danger for another. Eventually, my work took me to Manchuria, a province in the north-east of China. A little over a year after I arrived, the Japanese invaded. The village where I was working was attacked.'

He touched his scarred face. 'I received this and was lucky to escape with my life. It was then that I moved to Hong Kong. My career prospered there, and I became a canon in the Cathedral of St John.'

De Silva was puzzled. Telling his story had obviously cost Ryder a great deal of anguish. Why had he felt obliged to do so? What was the relevance to the case?

'Why are you returning to England?' he asked.

'I'm sick, Inspector. I have cancer. Doctor Brady will confirm it. He's kind enough to supply me with regular doses of morphine to keep the pain at bay. He also pays me the compliment of honesty and admits that I may not have long to live. My sister and I want to spend whatever time I have left with each other.'

'For a long time, I couldn't find out what had happened to my brother,' said Angela Meadows. 'He seemed to have vanished into thin air. It was the Church Missionary

Society who helped me in the end. I decided to leave Mrs Pilkington's employment and go to him, but when she found out why, she told me to wait and come with her on the trip she planned that winter. We didn't know George was ill at that stage. When he told me and said he wanted to see England one more time before it was too late, she insisted on paying his passage. I think she felt a particular sympathy because her late husband died of cancer.'

Now de Silva understood why Angela Meadows had said her employer was more generous than the casual observer would think. He addressed George Ryder.

'I have to ask you, sir; why have you told me all this? Isn't it a risk you didn't need to run?'

'Some would say so, Inspector, but I'm tired of concealment.'

Then the cleric gave him a searching look. 'There is someone else on this ship who has a reason for wanting Charles Pashley out of the way.'

'Yes?'

'Diana March.'

CHAPTER 22

From the far side of the Cabin Class lounge, Lady Caroline raised a slim hand and waved. Jane went to join her.

'Good afternoon, Lady Caroline.'

'Shall we take our stroll before tea? I think we have time.'

'I'd like that very much.'

On deck, a sharp breeze caught the broad brim of Lady Caroline's white sunhat. It was trimmed with violets that matched the colour of her calf-length chiffon dress. She clapped a hand to her head. 'I think the captain must be in more of a hurry than usual today,' she remarked. 'I expect he's anxious not to lose any more time. William says we already have done because of a fault with one of the engines, and we may have to join a later convoy than planned to go through the Suez Canal.'

'I'm looking forward to seeing the canal again.'

'Yes, it is a most impressive sight. I'm so pleased to have your company,' she added. 'William's very preoccupied with this dreadful business. It can't be helped, I know, but I must admit to feeling a little put out. I'd hoped that we would have a chance to relax and enjoy the journey together.'

'My husband's much the same,' said Jane sadly. 'If nothing has been resolved before we reach Port Said, I fear I may have difficulty persuading him to leave the ship.'

'Surely not? But then your husband does seem to be very dedicated to his duty. We shall have to make sure that William insists on relieving him of it.'

As if to stifle a cough, she raised a hand to cover her mouth. 'Oh dear,' she whispered. 'Here comes Clara Pilkington. I'm afraid she's seen us, and it's going to be hard to avoid her.'

'Lady Caroline! Good afternoon!'

Lumbering towards them, Mrs Pilkington had a wide smile on her face. The voluminous skirts of her pastel dress rippled in the wind. Her maid followed at a respectful distance bearing an armful of travelling rugs, a capacious handbag, and a small pile of books.

'So delightful to meet you,' she continued. 'I'm all alone this afternoon. I told Meadows I didn't need her.' She rolled her eyes. 'To tell the truth, I can't abide hearing that cough of hers for another minute.'

'I'm glad to say I've been very fortunate in being able to persuade Mrs de Silva to keep me company.'

Clara Pilkington raised the lorgnette she wore on a gold chain round her neck. Her expression resembled that of a sceptical farmer inspecting livestock at his local market. Jane returned a polite smile.

'How is your husband getting on with his investigations?' asked Mrs Pilkington.

'Making good progress, I believe.'

Mrs Pilkington harrumphed. 'You must tell him if he needs any advice that he's welcome to consult me.'

Jane saw a twinkle in Lady Caroline's eye. 'I wasn't aware you had experience of unmasking criminals, Mrs Pilkington.'

'Oh, not personally of course, but I read a great many detective novels, and one begins to have an instinct for these things.'

Jane would have liked to say that Shanti's instincts had been honed by real life, not just the pages of a book, but she decided to refrain.

'Of course, my husband and I knew dear Sir Arthur

Conan Doyle well. He often came to visit us at our home in London. Such a charming man, and an excellent sportsman as well as a talented writer. His way with words was unsurpassed. We had long talks about his work, and I flatter myself that my advice was a great help to him. He hinted that he would like to put me in one of his stories, but I said, "No, I never like to put myself forward".'

Jane suppressed a giggle and noticed that Lady Caroline's lips twitched. Fortunately, Clara Pilkington was too preoccupied with her reminiscences to notice.

After a little more conversation, they took their leave. 'I wonder if she really knew Sir Arthur Conan Doyle,' said Lady Caroline. 'If that story about his wanting to put her in a book is true, what a pity she turned him down. I'm sure he would have portrayed her in a most amusing way. Do you think she would have been the villain or the victim?'

Clara Pilkington's fluting voice interrupted them. 'Mrs de Silva, I nearly forgot. The singer fellow — the one who was found stabbed — I'm certain I saw him one evening with Mrs March. I'd come out after dinner to admire the stars with some of my dinner companions. The two of them were skulking in the shadows as if they didn't want to be seen, but very little passes me by.'

She sniffed. 'It seemed odd company to keep. I hope Emma Chiltern isn't going to be embarrassed by her prospective daughter-in-law.'

'I'm sure she hopes quite the reverse,' said Lady Caroline as Clara Pilkington waddled away.

Jane's brow creased. 'But she has given us something new to think about.'

'You must tell your husband, and I'll tell William. He won't be happy that the news of Delaney's murder has got out already. I can't imagine who told Mrs Pilkington.' She thought for a moment. 'I wonder if anyone has had a chance to look through Delaney's belongings. There might be something interesting there.'

'I don't expect there's been time, but I'm sure there will be.'

CHAPTER 23

De Silva frowned. 'What do you base this accusation on?'

'Diana March isn't her real name,' said George Ryder. 'When I first came across her, it was Sarah Betts. I can't say I knew her well, but at one time, she lived in the parish where my church was situated.'

'Did she have a connection to Charles Pashley?'

'For a while, yes. I used to see them about together. They were a striking couple and hard to miss. But Sarah wasn't the sort of young woman who'd endure scraping along if she didn't have to. She was trying to get on as an actress; she didn't have a lot of talent, but she had the looks. It was no surprise when she set her cap at one of the wealthy men who hung about the stage door. Eventually, she married him. We didn't see her around after that.'

'What happened to her husband?'

'He died. It was all over the papers at the time. They hadn't been married much more than a year when he fell down a steep flight of stairs and broke his neck. She claimed it was an accident. The police were suspicious and charged her with his murder, but she played the grieving widow, and the jury found her not guilty.' He gave a bitter laugh. 'You might say it was the performance of a lifetime.'

'How long ago would this have been?'

'I've been gone from England for eleven years. If I remember rightly, it happened about a year before I departed.'

With William Petrie's contacts, thought de Silva, it would be easy enough to check Ryder's story. If the case had been a sensation, it surprised him that no one on board seemed to have realised that Diana March was an impostor, but when he remarked on it to Ryder, the cleric shook his head.

'She's a clever woman, Inspector. She always contrived to hide her face behind a black veil when she was coming in or out of the courts. Only people in the courtroom would have seen her clearly. Her husband's family were well off, but they didn't move in high social circles. Her risk of being recognised by the denizens of Cabin Class would be minimal. Her appearance has changed considerably too. Far more sophisticated than when she was younger.'

'Polish paid for by her ill-gotten gains,' his sister muttered sourly.

Yet, she still took the precaution of changing her name and claiming she had never been to England before, thought de Silva. 'Do you think she remembers you?' he asked Ryder.

He shrugged. 'I doubt it very much. I don't imagine she took much notice of a humble clergyman in the first place, and now there are my scars. Most people avoid looking at me too closely, either out of tact or repugnance.'

But if she had a fling with Charles Pashley, de Silva was sure she would have remembered the journalist. Had he threatened to drop hints about her past in his dispatches home? According to Venetia de Vere and Angela Meadows, he was a spiteful man. He might have derived great pleasure from tormenting Diana March with the fear of exposure. But he was running ahead of himself. It was still possible that Ryder and his sister were blackening Diana March's character to serve their own ends. He needed to speak to William Petrie.

* * *

At the lobby to the Cabin Class section of the ship, the steward on duty waved de Silva through. They're getting to know me, he thought wryly. He no longer needed to produce his badge. At first, it had been just as well he had brought it with him; he had almost left it at home, but old habits die hard.

He sighed. The steward's recognition brought it home that he needed to find the solution to this case quickly and make it up to Jane for the unsatisfactory start to their holiday. Their plans to enjoy lazy days reading and chatting in the sun, interrupted only by the need to eat delicious meals, or perhaps play a few of the deck sports on offer had been rudely swept aside. He'd also looked forward to having the chance to have a good look at the Suez Canal and take some photographs as they went through it on the last stage of their journey to Port Said. If this investigation wasn't resolved by then, he doubted he'd have time to give Ferdinand de Lesseps' remarkable feat of engineering much of his attention.

There was no sign of William Petrie in the Cabin Class bar or any of the lounges. He would have to go to his stateroom and hope to find him there. But when he arrived at the door, he heard several voices inside and hesitated. If the Petries were entertaining guests, his intrusion wouldn't be welcome. Then he recognised Jane's voice. He raised his hand and knocked; a moment later, the door opened.

'Ah good, I was about to send someone to find you, de Silva.'

Petrie ushered him into the stateroom. He looked grim. 'The ladies have brought us some disturbing information. News of Delaney's murder has already leaked. Mrs Pilkington raised the subject. It's exactly what I didn't want to happen, and I intend to find out who's responsible.'

Doctor Brady's nurse came into de Silva's mind. She'd cared for Barbara Ross, and hadn't Mrs Meadows said she also attended Mrs Pilkington? He decided not to pin the blame on her on the strength of a hunch. There were more important things to deal with.

'But there's more,' Petrie continued. 'Why don't you explain, Mrs de Silva?'

Quickly, Jane went over the conversation with Clara Pilkington. 'If there was something between Diana March and Harry Delaney,' she finished, 'isn't it a clear indication she's not as innocent as she'd like people to think?'

'We'll need more than gossip to prove Diana March was involved in either of the murders, but we can make a start by getting on with the overdue job of looking through Delaney's belongings,' said Petrie. 'I've spoken to McDowell and found out what's been done with them. His passport's in safe keeping, but everything else was packed up and stowed away awaiting our arrival in England. McDowell gave instructions that, if the murderer isn't unmasked before then, it's all to be handed over to Scotland Yard. No one knows if there are relatives who need to be informed either. When Delaney signed on, he didn't offer the names of any next of kin. McDowell proposes to leave tracking them down, if they exist, to the Yard as well.'

'Are Delaney's belongings still stowed away?' asked de Silva.

'No, they're on their way here. I asked for them, so we can have a good look through everything. While we're waiting, you may as well tell us whether you found out anything relevant from Mrs Meadows.'

'I believe I did. Unexpected as it was, Mrs Meadows and Canon Ryder, who turn out to be brother and sister, proved to be a source of great enlightenment. Particularly in view of what my wife and Lady Caroline have learned.'

'We've only Ryder's and Meadows' word for it that Mrs

March has a murky past,' said William Petrie as de Silva came to the end of his story. 'We can't possibly accuse her without having cast-iron evidence in our possession. You may not think Arthur Chiltern's much of a force to be reckoned with, but the Chilterns are a very influential family. His father, Sir Robert, has the ear of the prime minister. If we're to accuse a woman who's about to become part of that family, we need to be absolutely sure of our ground.'

'Perhaps we will be after we've looked through Mr Delaney's belongings,' said Lady Caroline.

'I wish I shared your optimism, my dear.'

There were footsteps in the corridor and a knock on the door. William Petrie called out and a steward came in, weighed down by two leather cases that looked as if they had accompanied their owner on many journeys. The steward's face registered surprise as his glance took in the occupants of the room, but it soon reverted to a blank expression.

'Captain McDowell said I was to deliver these to you, sir. Where would you like them put?'

'Next to the door will do.' William Petrie fished in his pocket and brought out a few coins. He handed them to the steward. 'No need to mention this to anyone, do you understand?'

'Of course, sir.'

The steward pocketed the coins and smiled. 'Thank you, sir. Very generous of you.'

The door closed behind him. William Petrie rubbed his hands.

'So, what have we here? Mrs de Silva, will you and your husband take one? Lady Caroline and I will look through the other.'

The suitcase that the de Silvas were to search made a rustling sound as de Silva dragged it over the thick-pile carpet. With a grunt, he hoisted it onto a low table and snapped open the two brass catches. Throwing back the lid, he saw that the case contained a pile of old programmes from musicals, presumably ones that Delaney had been in. Jane pulled out a few and leafed through them to find cast lists.

'They're shows Delaney was in on Broadway. He looks to have been quite successful. Perhaps he kept them in the hope of impressing the producers of any new shows he wanted to get a part in.'

Delving into the case, de Silva found more. As he opened the top one, a newspaper cutting fluttered out.

'Only an assortment of clothes in this one,' Petrie was saying. 'But we'd better have them all out, I suppose.' He piled shirts, trousers, and underclothes on the floor and pushed them aside then began to run his hand over the lining of the case and into its interior pockets.

'Ah! What have we here?' He held up a packet of letters.

Lady Caroline took them from him. 'Poor man,' she said sadly. 'It seems hateful to pry into someone's private life like this.'

'Your sensitivity does you credit, my dear, but sometimes these things are unavoidable.'

'I know.'

Undoing the packet, she scanned the letters with a frown. 'They're from Mrs de Vere. Poor lady, she really was very smitten with Mr Delaney.'

'May I see them, Lady Caroline?' asked de Silva.

Lady Caroline handed him the letters. They were couched in the kind of flowery language he would have expected from Venetia de Vere, and they smelt of lilacs. He passed them on to William Petrie.

'There's nothing compromising here,' said Petrie when he reached the end. 'Mrs de Vere might be distressed to learn that Delaney had kept them, however. I wonder why he did.'

'Do you think he had some sinister motive?' asked his wife.

Petrie shrugged. 'You say she's well known as a writer. They might embarrass her if they were made public. Possibly he thought she'd be prepared to offer him something for their return. I suggest we don't inform her that they've been found. If she did have something to do with Delaney's murder, they provide evidence of a motive.'

He glanced at de Silva. 'You disagree?'

'They might indicate Mrs de Vere had a motive, but since the steward Ahmad confirmed her story that she didn't leave her cabin around the time of Delaney's murder, where was her opportunity?'

'A fair point.' Petrie looked down at the newspaper cutting on the floor.

'What's that?'

De Silva picked up the cutting and read out the headline: '*Fake Minister in Charity Fraud.* It's dated three years ago. A couple claiming to be an American Baptist minister and his wife raised money for a charity that turned out to be bogus.'

'Is there a photograph?' asked Petrie.

De Silva held out the cutting. 'A very blurry one.'

Petrie looked at the cutting. 'If it is Delaney, it's odd he kept it. Why would anyone do that?'

'Carelessness, perhaps.'

'Is there anything else for us to look at?'

'There's this letter.' Lady Caroline held it up. 'It's unsigned and the writing is different from the others. I think it may help us.'

She handed it to her husband. 'Would you read it out, dear?'

Clearing his throat, Petrie took the piece of paper.

'*Harry, please let's not quarrel. I beg you to forgive me. Now we're rid of Pashley, everything will be different. You need have no worries about A. If you want, we'll give up the plan and be together straight away. We can leave the ship at Port Said.*'

Petrie looked up. 'I can't read the next sentence. The ink is smudged, as if the writer shed a tear.'

'Or wanted Delaney to think they did,' said Jane.

Petrie smiled. 'You have the mind of a detective, Mrs de Silva.' He read on. '*Only you matter to me. You must decide for us both. Wait for me after midnight at the usual place.*'

Passing the letter to de Silva, William Petrie frowned. 'What do you make of that?'

The writing was certainly very different to Venetia de Vere's. Hers had been embellished with every possible flourish and curlicue, while the author of this letter had a much more angular style. The paper was plain; unlike Venetia de Vere's, it was unscented.

Petrie stood up. 'I need to clear my head. Will you join me in the bar, de Silva? Ladies, will you excuse us?'

'Of course.'

In the Cabin Class bar, Petrie led the way to a table in a quiet alcove. He signalled to a steward who hurried over. 'Whisky for me. The same for you, de Silva?'

'Thank you.'

'Difficult subject to discuss with ladies present,' said Petrie after the steward had gone to fetch the drinks. 'We only have Ryder's and his sister's word for it that Diana March has a past that she'd stick at nothing to conceal. They may be making up the whole story to throw us off the scent. For Ryder, revealing his past to us would be a small price to pay for saving his neck.'

A smartly dressed couple passed the table. He paused until they were out of earshot. 'That letter could have been written by a man or a woman,' he went on.

From the writing, it was plausible, thought de Silva; although was it really the way a man would express himself?

'From what we know of Ryder's past – there was a note of distaste in Petrie's voice – I wouldn't discount the possibility there was something between him and Delaney.

We know Pashley came back to his cabin in a bad state that night. What if Ryder put Delaney up to getting Pashley drunk? That would have allowed Ryder to finish the job later, when everything was quiet. Afterwards, they fell out, and Ryder needed to be rid of Delaney too.'

De Silva searched for a polite way of saying that this theory contained a lot of assumptions, and still didn't explain how Ryder had gained access to Pashley's cabin, but William Petrie wasn't to be stopped.

'The sister is called Angela, isn't she? She could be the "A" the letter mentions.'

Glancing at the steward weaving his way towards them balancing a silver tray carrying their drinks, Petrie was silent once more. The steward deposited two cut-glass tumblers of whisky and a clean ashtray on the table. It was made of brass in the shape of a tiny swimming pool with a svelte diver ready to plunge in. Beautifully designed, thought de Silva, like everything he had seen in Cabin Class.

Petrie pulled out his gold cigarette case – this time de Silva refused the offer of a cigarette. Petrie lit up. 'As for the plan, they might have had some idea of using Ryder's sister's connection with Clara Pilkington to defraud the old lady. Perhaps the original intention was to cut the sister in, but then Delaney rejected the idea.'

It was on the tip of de Silva's tongue to say that defrauding Mrs Pilkington was likely to be a considerable challenge, but he held back. Petrie might think the remark too familiar.

'If I may suggest, sir, I don't think we should rule out Mrs March yet. She might have written the letter, and if Ryder's telling the truth, she had as powerful a reason as he did for wanting to be rid of Pashley. The "A" could refer to Arthur Chiltern. No doubt she wouldn't want him to learn the details of her past.'

Petrie took a swallow of whisky. 'As I said before, de

Silva, the Chilterns are an influential family. If your theory's the correct one, we must have incontrovertible proof.' He tapped his cigarette over the ashtray, releasing a plug of glowing ash.

'Shouldn't we at least try to find out if Sarah Betts really exists?'

Reluctantly, Petrie nodded. 'Very well. My contact at Scotland Yard should be able to help us with that.'

CHAPTER 24

After de Silva and Petrie returned to the Petries' stateroom, Jane and de Silva left and went up to the Sun Deck. The first group of people they passed were drinking cocktails, laughing and talking noisily. De Silva winced, his head too full of speculation.

'Do you mind if we move somewhere else?'

'Of course not. It looks quieter down there.' Jane pointed to the far end of the deck. 'Now do tell me what Petrie wanted to say to you that we ladies couldn't be allowed to hear.'

'Was it so obvious?'

'It was rather, although Lady Caroline was too loyal to comment after you'd left us.'

As they walked, he explained. 'So,' he concluded, 'I can't disprove Petrie's theory any more than I can prove mine. I hope it won't take too long to get an answer from Scotland Yard.'

'If Diana March really is this woman Sarah Betts, her story about being born and brought up in Shanghai must be a sham.'

'Exactly.'

'I wonder where Sarah Betts went after she was acquitted of murdering her husband. Let's suppose Diana March wrote that letter to Harry Delaney, and it's true her real name's Sarah Betts. They might have been together a long

169

time. She may have been his accomplice in the charity fraud and other things as well.' She paused. 'Do you remember Lady Caroline mentioning that Diana March and Arthur Chiltern met through old friends in Hong Kong?'

'Now that you remind me, I do. What of it?'

'I was just thinking it would be interesting to know more about them, for example did they believe her story, or were they helping her to cover up her past? Presumably, Arthur Chiltern has no idea she may not be the person she claims to be.'

De Silva recalled Petrie saying that Chiltern's father had sent him to Hong Kong to put some backbone into him because he was worried his son was too naïve. Perhaps the experiment hadn't been such a success after all. If Diana March was determined to, she could easily fool an impressionable man who was dazzled by her.

He peered up at a flock of seagulls, wheeling high above the ship in the evening sky. 'It's not much further to go to Suez now. We'll be there tomorrow. Once we're through, there'll be only a couple more hours of sailing before we dock at Port Said. Then, there'll be nothing to stop the guilty party leaving the ship.'

'To say nothing of the fact that we want to disembark,' said Jane. She thought for a moment. 'If Mrs March and Canon Ryder aren't due to leave the ship there, wouldn't it be very suspicious if they did?'

'It would.'

'You could suggest to Petrie that he sends a message ahead to the police at Port Said. He'd need to describe all the suspects, then the police could station officers at every gangway and check if they disembarked.'

'What if they only went ashore for a little while?'

'They could be followed until they returned to the ship. It's not a perfect plan, but worth a try, surely?'

He considered the idea. 'It might work. I'll speak to Petrie.'

'You're not happy about leaving him in charge, are you?'

'I'm afraid I'm not. His attitude troubles me. Mrs March may be about to enter an important family – Petrie claims their connections go right up to the British prime minister – but there shouldn't be one law for the powerful and another for the rest. I was always taught that wasn't British justice.'

'Oh, I don't think you're being entirely fair. If the Chilterns are powerful, a mistake could cause Petrie a great deal of embarrassment, and at worst, it could damage his career. In view of that, he's bound to be very cautious, but I'm sure he wouldn't condone injustice.'

'I hope you're right, because my instincts tell me Canon Ryder is innocent. He didn't need to tell us about his past now that Pashley's dead, and his assertion that he's had enough of concealment seemed heartfelt.'

Jane thought for a moment. 'There is a way you might find out if what he told you is true. Also, William Petrie might be easier to sway if Doctor Brady confirms Ryder's illness.'

'Do you think Brady would speak to me about one of his patients?'

'It's worth asking.'

They reached the bow and leant on the ship's rail. Pressing his fingers into his temples to ease the ache in his head, de Silva closed his eyes for a few moments. He had an idea of his own, but was he bold enough to try it? He opened his eyes and looked at Jane. 'What's your plan?'

'After you both left us, I had a better look at that last letter. I noticed the writing sloped upwards towards the end of each line. It's a classic indication that the writer uses their left hand. It might be difficult to check whether Mrs March is left-handed, but simple enough where George Ryder's concerned.'

'How would you do that?'

'We've been properly introduced now, but I don't think he's made the connection between you and me.' She smiled. 'I think clergymen have to spend so much of their time being charming to the ladies in their congregation that we assume a kind of homogeneous form in their eyes.' She glanced over the rail at a greenish-brown mat of vegetation bobbing on the water. 'Like that seaweed over there.'

De Silva laughed. 'I hope not.'

She squeezed his arm. 'That's better. It's nice to hear you laugh. Now, back to George Ryder. I was talking to him at the service last Sunday. He told me about a book on the history of the Holy Land. All I need to do is ask him to write down the name of the author and the title, then watch which hand he uses. I'll go to the chapel service in the morning. He's almost certain to be there.'

'Good, and while you're about that, I can go and see Doctor Brady.'

Side by side, they gazed out to sea. The sky had taken on the translucent quality of a piece of fine porcelain. The hard blue of midday had faded to the delicate shade of a duck's egg, mingling with the palest of shell pinks in the west, where the sun was sinking towards the horizon. Once again, he thought what a pity it was that he could only take photographs in black and white.

'It so beautiful out here,' said Jane. 'We mustn't let these troubles spoil all this for us completely.'

He put an arm around her shoulders. 'You're right, we mustn't.'

'Just wait until you see the canal. I'm sure you'll be impressed. There's nowhere else like it. Miles and miles of desert sand stretching away on either side of this little ribbon of sea.'

He turned and smiled at her. 'I shall look forward to a geography lesson to distract me. And, I hope, more time to take pictures.'

Jane punched him gently in the ribs. 'The Cecil Beaton of Ceylon?'

'Something like that,' he said with a grin.

The upper reaches of the sky were indigo now. Below, the shell pink and pale blue had given way to fiery orange that picked out the crests of the darkening waves. Lights had gone on in windows and portholes. Inside, figures moved across the bright glass.

'We ought to go in,' said Jane. 'It must be time to dress for dinner.'

With a sensation of pleasure, de Silva realised he was hungry. At least his appetite was surviving the setbacks of the investigation.

Jane gave a little shiver. 'I remember how cold it was at night when we sailed through the desert on the way from England. The sky was so black, the stars looked like diamonds. We'll have to wrap up warmly if we want to come out and stargaze.'

He kissed her cheek. 'I'll be warm if I have you with me.'

Jane laughed. 'You are a silly, romantic old thing.'

'Is there anything wrong with that?'

'Nothing at all.'

CHAPTER 25

The next day, Jane was delighted to see George Ryder seated in the front pew at the regular service in the ship's chapel. Afterwards, he stayed to talk to the chaplain, and she seized her opportunity.

'What a lovely service,' she said, smiling at the chaplain.

'Good of you to say so, Mrs—'

'Oh, please call me Jane. I do so hate formality.'

'I particularly enjoyed the reading,' she went on. 'Such a thought-provoking passage. Don't you agree, Canon Ryder?'

Ryder murmured something and gave a polite nod. After a few more pleasantries, the chaplain excused himself to talk to another member of the congregation, and they were left alone.

'I've been trying to recall the title of the book we talked about last Sunday,' Jane began. The canon looked rather bemused. 'It was about the Holy Land,' she added helpfully.

'Ah, yes. *In the Steps of Saint Paul*. The author is H V Morton.'

'Oh dear, my memory is dreadful these days. I must write it down, or I shall probably have forgotten again by the time I reach my cabin.' She delved into the small handbag she carried and came out with a notebook. 'I've paper but nothing to write with. Do you happen to have a pen, Canon Ryder?'

He produced one from his top pocket and went to a

nearby table. Opening the notebook, he wrote down the title, using his right hand. As he returned the notebook to her, Jane gave him a beaming smile. 'How kind. I'll be sure to order a copy from the library as soon as I get home to England.'

* * *

'He's right-handed,' she said triumphantly, holding out the paper to de Silva. 'I'm sure he didn't write that letter. Have you managed to speak to Doctor Brady yet?'

'Not yet, he was busy, but I won't give up on him, and you've made a good start.'

Jane sat down in the cabin's other armchair. 'Thank you, dear. Now, what else can we do? There must be something.'

De Silva rested his chin on his hand. After he'd found he had to wait to see Brady, he'd been mulling over his options. He could do nothing and let matters take their course. If William Petrie had his way, that was likely to result in George Ryder being accused, perhaps wrongly, of at least one, if not both murders. If that happened, when they reached England, he would go to trial. It appeared to be the case that he was travelling Cabin Class thanks to Mrs Pilkington. De Silva would have been surprised if he was more than comfortably off. He was unlikely to be able to afford a top defence counsel, and even if he did get the money, what if the jury turned against him? When even a fundamentally good man like William Petrie showed some prejudice, it had to be a real concern.

'I want to find out more about Diana March,' he said. 'I know Petrie's reluctant, but that can't be helped. If George Ryder was telling the truth, she has a clear motive for wanting Pashley dead. And that letter lends itself to the interpretation that she and Harry Delaney were involved with each other in committing the murder, just as much as it does to Petrie's theory. The question is, given the risk of incurring Petrie's displeasure, how far am I prepared go?'

He levered himself out of his armchair. 'I need some fresh air. Would you like a stroll before lunch?'

'That would be nice.'

After a turn around the Promenade Deck, they climbed the stairway to the Sun Deck above. Tables and chairs had been set out, shaded by brightly coloured parasols. Stewards wove between them bringing drinks to the passengers ensconced there.

'By this time tomorrow, we could be at Port Said,' said Jane. 'I hear there's to be a grand ball in Cabin Class tonight to celebrate the ship's passage from Asia into Africa, but some people seem to have decided to start their celebrations early.'

She shaded her eyes. 'Shanti? You're plotting something. I can tell.'

'I'm going to search Mrs March's cabin. She and Arthur Chiltern are bound to be going to the ball tonight. That gives me my chance.'

Jane frowned. 'Oh Shanti, I hope this is wise.'

He shrugged. 'It's risky, but can you think of a better time?'

'No,' she said after a moment's thought. 'But how will you get in?'

'I'll have to get the pass key off old Ahmad. If memory serves, all the keys are kept on one ring. I'll tell him I need to check something in Pashley's cabin and just hope he doesn't decide to come to see what I'm doing. If I leave it until late in the evening, he'll probably be more interested in dozing in his little cubby hole than watching me to check which cabin I go to.'

'But what if he only gives you the key to Pashley's cabin?'

'I'll have to take something with me, so I can pick the

lock on Mrs March's door. As there's always a steward on duty, I doubt the cabin door locks are very complicated. One of your hairpins ought to do the job.'

CHAPTER 26

'Very well, I'll alert the police at Port Said and ask them to send some men to patrol the gangways after we dock.'

From the depths of his armchair in the Cabin Class bar, William Petrie fixed de Silva with a stern look. 'But don't forget, I insist on caution. I don't want you doing anything rash.'

'I understand, sir.' That was a sufficiently neutral remark, thought de Silva.

Petrie rubbed a sunburnt hand across his forehead. 'I'll be dashed glad to have this over. I expect you feel the same. You and your wife can carry on with your holiday and forget all about it.' He looked at his watch. 'I promised Lady Caroline I'd take her up on deck to see the ship entering the canal, but there's time for a quick one.'

De Silva accepted another whisky. Petrie was talking about the canal. How it had taken ten years to build, and the work had mostly been done by hand, using tens of thousands of labourers. De Silva spared a thought for them, working in the blazing sun and no doubt poorly paid and housed. It was one of the unpalatable aspects of progress.

As Petrie droned on about tonnages and transits, de Silva remembered he had been a naval man during the war. He let his mind drift to his task that evening. The ball was due to begin at ten o'clock. He had better start a little later than that in case Mrs March came back to her cabin to refresh her hair or her make-up between the dinner and the dancing.

The table shifted slightly, and he returned to the present. Petrie had finished his drink and was standing up. 'I'd better be getting along. Thank you for your help, de Silva. Even if this business isn't concluded before you leave us at Port Said, I'll see to it that Archie Clutterbuck knows you're due some of the credit.'

CHAPTER 27

'How did it go?' asked Jane.

'He agreed to arrange for the police to patrol the gangways at Port Said.'

'That's good, isn't it?'

All at once, de Silva felt very weary. What if he was wrong, and he was caught this evening?

'Shanti?'

He sighed. 'We may be on the wrong track with Diana March, you know.'

'No, I'm becoming more convinced that we aren't.'

He frowned. 'Why?'

'Because these were delivered while you were out.' She picked up a brown envelope that had been neatly slit with a paper knife.

'What's in there?'

'Your photographs. The film you gave to James Ross has come back from being developed by the official photographer.'

De Silva felt a prickle of interest. 'I'd forgotten all about that. How do the photographs help?'

'I'll show you. There's one that I think you'll be very interested in.'

She took the photographs out of the envelope and arranged them neatly on the coffee table. 'Look at this one,' she said, pointing to it.

'The bazaar at Bombay? What's so special about it?'

'Take a closer look.'

He frowned. 'It's a bit fuzzy. I shall have to learn to keep the camera steadier.'

Jane reached for her sewing bag and brought out the little magnifying glass she used when a piece of embroidery required particularly small stitches. 'Look at it through this: the left-hand side of the picture.'

At first, he saw nothing out of the ordinary, just the frontage of a small hotel shaded by palm trees. A woman selling mangoes squatted beside the steps leading up to the porch while her child played nearby in the dust.

'I don't see anything unusual.'

'Look again.'

Then he saw them: a man and a woman. The shade from the palm trees blurred their faces, but they were still discernible.

He put down the magnifying glass. 'Harry Delaney and Diana March. So that was where he was going when he pushed past us in the bazaar.'

Jane smiled triumphantly. 'When he sees that, Petrie can't deny there's a connection between them, and I think you're entitled to do whatever's necessary to find out what it is.'

It might provide them with the key to solving Pashley's murder, thought de Silva, as he dressed for dinner. But if Harry Delaney was the person who had conspired with Diana March to murder Charles Pashley, why would she subsequently want to be rid of him? It seemed a reasonable assumption that they were lovers, and if the date of the newspaper cutting about the American Baptist minister and his wife was anything to go by, they might have been together for at least three years.

De Silva cast about for answers. There was Delaney's erratic behaviour in the bazaar at Bombay, and later, in the dining room on the ship when he had knocked into one of the tables and charged off with no apology. Then there was the cocaine found in his pocket when his corpse was discovered. Was Diana March afraid her lover was becoming a liability and endangering her plans, whatever they might be?

* * *

Clouds marbled the sky, and searing heat rolled off the desert robbing the sea air of freshness. The *Jewel of the East* lay at anchor. She had been idle for two hours, waiting with a fleet of ships of all shapes and sizes for the signal for their convoy to enter the canal.

'The entrance is less dramatic than I expected,' de Silva remarked to Jane. 'Water disappearing into a flat landscape doesn't make for a very stirring sight.'

'It would have been more dramatic if a Frenchman called Bartholdi had had his way. He wanted to set up a huge statue of an Egyptian peasant girl at the entrance to the canal. She would have symbolised free navigation and trade.'

'Why did he fail?'

'He wanted too much money, so the Suez Canal company turned him down. He didn't give up though. Eventually, he managed to sell his idea to America, and his Egyptian peasant became the Statue of Liberty that stands in New York Harbour.'

De Silva smiled. 'The things you know, my love.'

'Don't forget, it was my job to know things once.'

He felt a jolt, and the smell of engine oil wafted towards him. Plumes of smoke began to rise again from the fore and aft funnels. 'We must be getting ready to move off,' he said.

Jane smiled. 'Camera at the ready?'

'Of course, I don't intend to do without photographs to remind us of how we went through the famous Suez Canal.'

Gradually, the ships formed into a line then the leading one nosed into the entrance to the canal, and the rest followed. De Silva felt the hot wind on his face and saw the ochre desert slip by on either side. The emptiness was interrupted at intervals by unremarkable buildings huddled close to the water bank. The sight was far less romantic than he had expected, but at sunset, the beauty of the desert was revealed. The sands took on every shade of russet and crimson. As dusk approached, shadows deepened, sharply defining the dunes, and lights twinkled in the buildings, giving them a festive air.

De Silva put away his camera and buttoned his jacket. 'I think I have enough pictures now. Anyway, it's getting too dark for them to come out well.'

The temperature was already dropping. Other passengers had begun to drift inside. He looked at his watch. Soon it would be time to change for dinner, but he doubted he would enjoy it much, his mind too fixed on the search he had to make. He was still worried something would go wrong, or he would find nothing. He needed all the ammunition he could get before he tackled Petrie again. He remembered Doctor Brady; he'd neglected to follow up questioning him about George Ryder's health. Maybe he would be lucky and find the good doctor available now.

* * *

'Doctor Brady has almost finished his evening surgery, Inspector,' said the nurse de Silva remembered from the evening Delaney had been found dead. 'If you don't mind waiting, I'm sure he'll spare you a few moments.'

De Silva thanked her and sat down. Ten minutes passed before she reappeared.

'Doctor Brady will see you now, Inspector.'

Brady's consulting room was as neat as a new pin. The shelves behind him displayed a range of daunting-looking medical tomes, and numerous framed certificates attesting to his qualifications in various branches of medicine hung on the walls. De Silva noticed their most recent date was twenty years ago.

'What can I do for you?' Brady asked, picking up a pen and rotating it between a thumb and finger. 'I hope neither you nor Mrs de Silva are under the weather.'

'Both in the best of health, thank you. It's the Pashley case I'd like to discuss.'

Brady frowned. 'I don't think I've anything to add, so I doubt I'll be of much help, but fire away.'

When de Silva had explained his interest in Canon Ryder, Brady looked at him shrewdly.

'Under normal circumstances, I would refuse to divulge personal information about my patients, but as you've asked me in an official capacity, I'm prepared to make an exception. Yes, I can tell you that Canon Ryder is a very sick man. What I can't tell you is how long he'll live. At present, I'm able to keep pain at bay for him, but when that changes, his decline is likely to be swift. Indeed, in these situations, it's usually a blessing for the patient when that's the case.'

He leant back in his chair and steepled his hands. 'Does that help you, Inspector?'

'It certainly does. Thank you.'

CHAPTER 28

There was dancing for the Tourist Class passengers after dinner. De Silva and Jane stayed until eleven then slipped away, back to their cabin. When he had tucked the items that he needed for his mission in his pocket, he kissed her cheek. 'Wish me luck.'

'Good luck, dear,' she whispered.

The old steward, Ahmad, was in the cubby hole at the end of the corridor when de Silva arrived.

'I need to check something in Mr Pashley's cabin,' he said. 'Give me the key, would you? Doctor Brady has the third one and the other is still missing.'

Stiffly, Ahmad got to his feet and shuffled to the key rack on the back wall. He reached down the large ring that held the pass keys to all the cabins on the corridor and started to try and unclip it with his arthritic hands.

'No need for that,' said de Silva quickly. 'I see each one's labelled. I'll take them as they are.'

'Thank you, sir.'

De Silva drew a deep breath; the first hurdle was overcome. But as he walked down the corridor, he heard a door open. His heart beat faster. Had he miscalculated? If Diana March came out, he'd need to be very plausible if he was to convince her that nothing was wrong. Quickly, he turned aside to Charles Pashley's cabin and searched the ring for the key.

Diana March's maid emerged, carrying an armful of dresses. She stopped and gave him a wary look. 'Good evening, sir,' she faltered.

'Good evening.'

The dress at the bottom of the pile dislodged itself, putting the rest in danger of falling on the floor. He stepped forward and helped her to rearrange the armful then stood back.

She flushed. 'Thank you.'

'My pleasure. Don't let me detain you. I have a few things to see to in here.'

Her wary expression became timid. 'Please sir, they're saying in the laundry that the gentleman who had that cabin was killed. Do you think we're safe if the killer's not been caught?'

Half the ship probably knew what had happened by now, de Silva thought with irritation. 'You have no need to worry,' he said firmly. 'The culprit will be apprehended soon.'

The maid thanked him but didn't look much reassured. As she walked away down the corridor, he went into Pashley's cabin, waiting with the door ajar until he was confident that she'd gone. His heartbeat had returned to its normal rate by the time he was ready to carry on with his task.

The drawing room of Diana March's cabin was as immaculate as he remembered. He slipped on the gloves he had brought with him – he didn't want to leave any telltale finger marks on the highly polished furniture – and started his search.

In a short time, he had established that there was nothing of interest and moved on to the bedroom. This was an equally immaculate room. Inside the long wardrobe that took up one wall, rows of glamorous dresses in chiffons and silks were precisely spaced on the rails. Next to them were shelves filled with neatly folded silk blouses, cashmere wraps, and lace-trimmed underwear. There were elbow-length gloves for evening wear, wrist-length ones made of soft kid for day, and silk scarves in a variety of colours and patterns. Below were hatboxes and dozens of pairs of shoes for different occasions.

He turned his attention to the dressing table: a kidney-shaped one with a fall of gold brocade draping from the glass top. This was less tidy, and he had to be careful not to knock over any of the bottles and pots of perfume and make-up. To one side was a lacquered Chinese box. He tried the catch; it was unlocked.

The red-velvet interior contained a gold necklace, a bracelet, and a pair of pearl-drop earrings. He recalled the diamonds Diana March wore when he first saw her on the evening that he and Jane had been invited to dinner by the Petries. Presumably, she was wearing them tonight.

He lifted the top tray and found several more bracelets underneath, as well as a plain gold ring. It seemed a very modest piece of jewellery for Mrs March. He took it out and examined it, but there was no inscription.

Replacing the trays, he was about to close the box when it occurred to him that it was unusually deep for what it contained. He tapped the bottom with his knuckles. It gave off a hollow sound. He removed the trays once more and looked at the red velvet closely. There was a tiny, loose tab of material in one corner. He pinched it between his thumb and forefinger and pulled. The false base yielded with one easy motion, to reveal a few folded sheets of paper underneath.

He glanced at his watch, he had been there twenty minutes. Out of caution, he left the box and went to the drawing room. He opened the door a fraction and listened. The corridor was quiet, but he didn't want to risk taking much longer. After midnight, some of the occupants of the cabins might return and hear him moving about, or old Ahmad might begin to wonder what was taking him so long and come to investigate.

Back in the bedroom, he looked at what he'd found. There were no letters, only what looked to be drafts for newspaper articles. They were all in the same handwriting and signed by Charles Pashley. He checked the dates. One was dated for the day Pashley had been found dead. Here was the answer to the puzzle about why he'd found no dispatch for that morning in Pashley's cabin. Diana March had somehow intercepted it along with these others.

Quickly, he memorised the relevant points. It surprised him that Diana March had kept the articles. Presumably, she'd had no fear of being found out. Lucky for him, of course. He began to repack the box, but as he did so, one of the pearl earrings rolled off its velvet cushion and onto the thickly carpeted floor. Bending to retrieve the piece, he noticed that one of the pearl drops was missing from the end of its thin, gold wire. He looked around the floor, as a precaution even running the palm of his hand over the carpet, but nothing bounced up from the thick pile. The pearl must have already been broken off, and he hadn't noticed it when he first opened the box.

He finished the job and snapped the catch shut. Another glance at his watch told him it was nearly midnight; he must hurry. Ten minutes later, the keys were returned, and he was back with Jane in their cabin.

'I'm certain those articles were intended for the newspaper Charles Pashley wrote for,' he said.

'I wonder how Mrs March got hold of them. It's easy to see why she wanted to. From what you've told me, there are some very broad hints in them about her past, and each one is more explicit than the last.'

'I'll have to check with the radio officer whether reports were sent out under Pashley's name on those days. If they were, I'd be very interested to know the contents.'

'Do you think Mrs March would have written them herself and substituted them for the ones we have here?'

'Very likely. She could have copied Pashley's writing so as not to raise the radio officer's suspicions. Provided the newspaper didn't raise any queries, Pashley wouldn't have any idea that his own reports weren't getting through. The ruse would work perfectly until the ship docked at Port Said. Then there would be a risk that a recent newspaper made its way on board.'

'In other words, she needed to deal with Pashley before then. We're left with the question of who supplied her with the reports. The steward, Chung, do you think?'

He nodded. 'It would have been a moment's work to push them under her door after he'd collected them from Pashley early in the morning. The only risk would be that Pashley departed from his routine and didn't have one ready until everyone was up and about. It would have been harder for Chung to deliver it then, giving March hardly any time to concoct her own version and tell Chung to take it to the radio office if she needed to.'

Jane laughed. 'A clever woman would have had a supply ready.'

'The agility of your criminal mind is impressive, my love. I'll question Chung again in the morning. If he has any sense, he'll realise it's not worth holding anything back now.'

'If Diana March is the murderer, do you think Chung gave her the key to Pashley's cabin?'

'Possibly, but it doesn't explain why Pashley came back incapacitated that night. We know Pashley was drinking in the Tourist Class bar that evening. What we don't know is who he was with. The one drink he bought, according to the account ledger, wouldn't be enough to make him drunk. Either someone was plying him with more, or they slipped something into his glass. I'm beginning to have an idea who that person was.'

'Harry Delaney?'

'Yes.'

'It fits, doesn't it? He could have been conspiring with Diana March to make sure Pashley was out cold by the time he went to bed. Then under the guise of helping him downstairs, Delaney steals the key to the cabin, so Pashley has to ask Chung to let him in with the pass key.' She frowned. 'There's still a catch. How did Delaney give the key to Diana March?'

'Did he? If Chung's been lying all along, Delaney might be the killer, and Chung is covering up for him.'

'But then why murder Pashley in his cabin? There must be other places where he could have done the deed unobserved.'

De Silva rubbed the bridge of his nose with a crooked forefinger and yawned. 'I can't answer that, and I'm exhausted. Time for bed. We need to be up again in a few hours.'

'I'll set the alarm for six.'

CHAPTER 29

The alarm clock shrilled. De Silva forced open a bleary eye then closed it and turned over to bury his head in the pillow. He just needed another hour.

A gentle shake of his shoulders told him that Jane was already awake. 'You have to get up, dear,' she whispered. 'There's a lot to do.'

With a groan, he hauled himself up and swung his legs over the side of the bed. His head feeling heavy, he lumbered to the bathroom and found toothbrush and toothpaste. Teeth vigorously scrubbed, he felt a little better. He splashed cold water on his face, rubbed it dry with a towel, then dragged a comb through his hair. That would do; he wasn't going to a party.

Jane was dressed and ready for the day. As he pulled on his own clothes, he ran over in his mind the questions he wanted to ask Chung.

Breakfast was being prepared when de Silva arrived in the kitchen quarters. The smell of coffee, kippers, and frying bacon induced a pang of hunger. Sweating kitchen staff pushed trolleys laden with platters of fruit and mounds of pastries. Two kitchen porters passed him carrying a huge, double-handled cauldron bubbling with porridge.

He found the officer in charge and asked for Chung to be brought to a room where they could speak privately. Waiting for him, de Silva tapped an impatient rhythm on the table top. He needed answers from the man quickly. Unless they were held up as they exited the canal, there were only two more hours before they would be out of it and into the Mediterranean Sea. After that, it would take about the same length of time to reach Port Said and, he hoped, the local police officers.

When the door opened, and Chung saw who waited for him, he tried to turn and run. The officer who had brought him in grabbed him. Twisting his arm behind his back, he propelled him into the room and pushed him into a chair.

'The police are coming on board at Port Said,' said de Silva. 'If you're to have a chance of avoiding being handed over to them, you'd better answer me truthfully. No holding anything back this time.'

Chung's head dropped. 'Yes, sir.'

'Were you stealing the messages you collected from Mr Pashley each night and giving them to Mrs March?'

Chung's bowed head nodded.

'What happened after that?' There was silence. 'Look at me,' snapped de Silva.

The steward looked up reluctantly. 'She would tell me to come back in half an hour. She would give me back the message and tell me to take it to the radio room as usual.'

'Would the messages always be the same ones as you'd brought her?'

'I don't know, sir. They were always in an envelope.'

De Silva drew his own conclusions.

'What else did she tell you to do for her?'

'She said I must tell no one that she sometimes left her cabin late at night. If I did, she'd see to it I lost my job.'

'Did you lie about their movements for anyone else? If you want to change your story, you'd better do it now.'

Chung shook his head. 'No, sir, everything else was the truth.' He shivered. 'Will I be able to stay on the ship? I have a family. If I lose my job, they'll have nothing.'

De Silva felt some sympathy for him. Chung had been a fool, but a hard life never made for good decisions. Now that the fellow was cooperating, maybe he would put in a good word for him, but ultimately, the decision would be in Captain McDowell's hands.

'You should have considered the risks in the first place,' he said sharply. 'The captain will decide.'

He nodded to the officer. 'Keep him here for the moment. He may have something to eat, but he must talk to no one. I'll send a message when he's allowed to go back to work.'

* * *

The next stop was the ship's radio office. He reached it a little before eight o'clock, and it was already humming with activity. When he showed his badge to the chief radio officer and explained his connection to William Petrie, the man nodded.

'If you'll wait here, sir, I'll see if we still have any of Mr Pashley's instructions. If the dispatches you're interested in are only a few days old, they may still be here. We usually keep them for a while in case of any queries.'

He returned from a back room with several pieces of paper. 'These are all we have, sir. If you need to take them with you, I'd be obliged if you'd sign for them.'

De Silva put his signature to the form the officer prepared and hurried back to their cabin. Jane looked up as he came in. 'Did you have any luck?'

'Yes, look at these.'

They read the dispatches together.

'You must go to William Petrie straight away,' said Jane when they'd finished. 'Every reference to Diana March or hint about her in the ones you found in her cabin has been removed. She obviously rewrote Pashley's originals to suit her own ends.'

'What, go now? He might not even have breakfasted.'

The determined expression with which he was very familiar came over Jane's face. 'If he hasn't, his eggs and bacon will have to wait. This is important.'

The steward on duty at the entrance to Cabin Class didn't recognise him, so for once, he had to show his badge. Petrie's door was opened by his manservant.

'Mr Petrie is not able to receive visitors at this hour, sir.'

De Silva raised his voice to a carrying tone. 'Please send my apologies for disturbing him, but it's imperative that I see him without delay.'

'Who is it?' Petrie sounded irritable.

'Your name, sir?' asked the manservant.

'Inspector de Silva.'

'Oh, let him in.'

Attired in a burgundy silk dressing gown with gold facings, William Petrie sat at a table laid up for breakfast. Fragrant steam rose from a silver coffee pot, cut-glass dishes held English marmalade and neat curls of butter. There was a rack of appetisingly browned toast.

His fork hovering over a plate of bacon and eggs, Petrie scowled. 'Drat it, de Silva. This is a bit early, isn't it? Lady Caroline's not even up yet. What's so important that you need to see me at this hour?'

Putting out of his mind the thought that he would have liked some of that coffee to fortify himself, de Silva embarked on the story of his recent findings, beginning with the photograph of Diana March and Delaney, and the most important find of all: the evidence that Diana March had been doctoring Charles Pashley's newspaper articles.

By the time he reached the end, Petrie had pushed away his half-eaten plate of eggs and bacon. He got up from his chair. 'You certainly know how to spoil a perfectly good breakfast, de Silva. I'll need to think about this. I'm still not convinced we can rule Canon Ryder out, whether he committed the crimes with or without the involvement of his sister.'

When de Silva explained what he had learnt from Doctor Brady about Ryder's prospects, Petrie gave a grudging nod. 'I'll take that into account.' He called his manservant who had been out of the room. De Silva wondered how much he had overheard.

'Order some fresh coffee for Inspector de Silva, and whatever else he'd like, then come and shave me and help me dress.'

'Very well, sir.'

A short while later, de Silva was savouring an excellent cup of coffee and munching marmalade on toast. He felt considerably more cheerful than he had when he arrived in Petrie's stateroom, yet a sense of apprehension hadn't left him. Was Petrie going to be difficult? What would be his strategy then?

Petrie emerged from the bedroom, immaculate in navy blazer and fawn trousers. 'Lady Caroline bids you good morning by the way,' he said. 'Very well, you've introduced enough doubt into my mind. We'd better talk to Mrs March.' He rubbed a hand over his smooth chin, glowing from his shave. 'I'll have to think of the best way of approaching her. Can't just go and bang on her door. I'd rather not cause a commotion.'

He turned to his manservant. 'Take a message asking if she'll visit Lady Caroline this morning. We'll hope that does the trick. If not, we'll have to think of another way.'

Conversation died as they waited. De Silva wished William Petrie was less circumspect. He would have preferred to catch their quarry off guard.

When half an hour passed, and the servant didn't return, Petrie frowned. 'What's keeping the man? De Silva, you'd better go and see what's going on.'

At the entrance to the corridor where Diana March's stateroom was situated, the servant's expression immediately revealed that all was not well.

'Mrs March isn't there, Inspector.'

'Does anyone know where she is?'

'Her maid may know something, sir. She's been fetched to Mrs March's stateroom. Will you come and speak to her?'

The maid de Silva had run into the previous evening looked up with frightened eyes as he stepped inside. One of her cheeks was badly bruised.

'What happened?' asked de Silva with a frown. He had a nasty feeling he could guess.

'She said I'd broken her earring, sir. One of the pearl ones. I said I hadn't, but she said who did then, and what was I doing snooping around in her jewellery box? I said I didn't know anything about that.'

The girl started to cry. 'She got really nasty and slapped me,' she said shakily. 'She said I was lying. It just came out, sir. I told her I'd seen you in the corridor when I was taking her dresses out to be pressed. Maybe you had something to do with it. She wanted to know what you looked like. When I told her, she sent me back to my quarters and told me not to show my face again until she sent for me.'

'Are any of your mistress's clothes missing?'

'I don't know, sir. Shall I look?'

'Yes, please.'

The maid wiped her eyes and went into the bedroom. She returned a few minutes later. 'No, sir.'

'I expect you know her wardrobe pretty well.'

'Yes.'

'Has anything at all gone missing recently?'

The maid paused for a moment, thinking. 'She lost a cloak and a pair of gloves a few days ago. I asked if I should look for them, but she told me not to bother. They'd probably turn up, and anyway, she didn't much care for them.'

'Can you remember exactly when that was?'

'Three or four days. I'm not sure.'

De Silva groaned silently. If that was what Diana March had used to cover herself up when she stabbed Delaney, the cloak and gloves were probably at the bottom of the sea by now. She'd probably had another disguise ready for when she left the stateroom this morning. She knew they were onto her, and they didn't have long to find her.

CHAPTER 30

Occupied with organising the search, de Silva hardly noticed the ship's exit from the canal into the Mediterranean Sea. The searchers combed cabins and storerooms, public rooms, and the crew's quarters. Even the lifeboats had their tarpaulins lifted to make sure that Diana March hadn't sought refuge in one of them.

'What I'd like to know,' said Petrie, 'is how she managed to get to the storeroom to kill Delaney. I think I'll have a word with Arthur Chiltern. We can't keep him in the dark for ever. I suggest you speak to that steward Ahmad.'

Arthur Chiltern thought he remembered his fiancée leaving the ballroom after dinner, saying she had a headache and wanted to rest for a while. 'He thinks it was about midnight,' said Petrie, 'but he can't remember precisely what time she came back. Naturally, the poor fellow was very cut up, so it was hard to get a lot of sense out of him. What did the steward have to say for himself?'

'He swears she didn't return to her stateroom that evening before she came back with Arthur Chiltern. I'm afraid he wasn't sure what time she left this morning. The old fellow admits he might have dozed for a bit.'

'Most unfortunate.'

'I also checked with the steward who was on duty in the ballroom lobby. He recalls that when she left for a while during the party, Mrs March collected a cloak. He particularly remembers it because the cloak had been left behind a few evenings previously, and they'd been waiting for someone to claim it. However, he doesn't think she came back wearing it when she returned to the ballroom later.'

'What's the relevance?'

De Silva explained about the missing cloak and gloves. 'I believe that having arranged to meet Delaney in the storeroom, she used them to protect the rest of her clothing when she stabbed him. I expect they're at the bottom of the sea by now,' he finished.

'How would she get to the storeroom unnoticed?'

'There are a few stairways on deck that the crew use to go between Cabin Class and Tourist Class. They're only roped off, and Diana March doesn't seem the kind of woman who'd be afraid of taking a risk.'

* * *

'No sign of her,' de Silva said wearily when he took a break to report to Jane and gulp down a glass of iced tea in the lounge.

'I'm sure someone will spot her if she tries to leave the ship at Port Said.'

'I hope so. But she's a clever woman. If she's managed to elude us on board, I wouldn't like to guarantee that she won't give us the slip when we dock. I hope these Port Said police know their job.'

He thought of the bustle down in Third Class, by far the busiest area of the ship. Searches had been carried out there, and they had turned up nothing, but it would be easy to lie low in those crowded conditions. He wished they had more time. He ran a finger round inside his collar. It was humid, and all this rushing around made him sweat. The stench of engine oil was still in his nostrils from his forays into the bowels of the ship to find out if any progress had been made down there.

As they went out on deck to see if the city had come into view, seagulls whirled in raucous flocks, a cascade of white in the electric blue sky. It seemed to de Silva that their cries mocked his efforts; he gave them a hostile glance. Not far away across the water, sunlight gleamed on the waterfront buildings of Port Said. Minarets stabbed the sky, and a maze of buildings stretched into the distance, some low, others many storeys high. De Silva knew that those buildings and the streets snaking through them would be crammed with inhabitants. It would be easy for someone to disappear in this Tower of Babel.

'Good, I've found you.' William Petrie appeared at their side. 'The Port Said police have their instructions. They'll arrest Mrs March – or Sarah Betts if that's really her name – if she tries to leave the ship.'

De Silva didn't feel confident. There were many gangways to patrol, and people tended to merge into an amorphous stream of humanity. 'I suggest we post men with binoculars above the gangways, sir.'

'Good idea. I'll speak to McDowell.'

The plaintive call of a muezzin drifted across the water; the city shimmered in the heat. De Silva felt a tightening in the pit of his stomach as he heard the engines cut. There was a blast from the horn as the ship edged onto her moorings. Ropes secured her, and gangways rumbled out.

De Silva saw an officer go ashore to greet a group of uniformed men. Presumably they were the police William Petrie had sent ahead for. After a short conversation, they fanned out to the bottoms of the gangways. He hoped there were going to be enough of them to do the job. It would take a little time for the port authority to send officials on board to clear the ship for disembarkation, then the fun would begin.

CHAPTER 31

Sarah Betts studied herself in the mirror above the basin in the cleaners' room. Her face was bare of make-up, and an unflattering net plastered her hair to her head – Diana March no longer existed.

She stretched to ease the ache from the round-shouldered posture she had adopted all day and swung her arms. No one had taken any notice of the drab cleaner dusting tables and sweeping floors in the crew's quarters since dawn. She had kept her head down and avoided conversation. It wasn't the first time that the lazy-minded assumptions people made about others had served her well.

In the toilet cubicle, she removed her pinafore, put the nondescript brown coat over her dress and buttoned it to the throat. She peeled away the hairnet and replaced it with a shabby felt hat, then kicked off the flat, baggy shoes she wore. With sudden dismay, she looked at the ones she had planned to replace them with. She hadn't thought about it before, but they were too obviously new and expensive. She looked again at the ones she had just discarded; they were so shabby, they might raise suspicion in another way.

Feeling a twinge of annoyance, she opened the Gladstone bag. It contained her few possessions, including a forged passport and a small toilet bag that held, among other things, a nail file. She took off one shoe and scraped at it with the file, paying the most attention to the toe and the heel. That was better; she began to mete out the same treatment to the other shoe.

When Charles Pashley joined the ship at Calcutta, she'd realised he might need to be dealt with, and insisted that she and Delaney made plans in case they came under suspicion. He'd gone ashore at Colombo and bought old clothes for them both. Back on the ship, he'd stolen a set of cleaner's overalls.

At first, he'd kept what they needed in his cabin, but over the next few days, she'd smuggled the bag holding the clothes she would wear into her stateroom and hidden it at the back of the cupboard where lifejackets were stored. Luckily, the description Delaney had given her of the crew areas had been good enough for her to find her way around without raising suspicion. She had also been able to find a place to stow away what she didn't immediately want to wear.

The nail file tucked away, she patted the bag. The purse inside contained all the money she had. With his boasting about how much that old fool Venetia de Vere had lavished on him, she'd expected there to be more in Delaney's wallet. She'd left the ring – the monogram on it would have made it too recognisable. Anyway, it probably wasn't worth much. Her real insurance lay elsewhere. Under her corset, she felt against her skin the cool pressure of the jewellery Arthur had given her. To avoid attracting attention, she would start by selling the least valuable pieces.

She stuffed the clothes she didn't need into the rubbish bin in the corner of the cubicle and drew a deep breath. Time to leave.

At the top of the gangway, she paused to let a woman struggling with heavy luggage, a baby, and a toddler go ahead. Her clothes looked cheap, and her hair was greasy. Sarah hooked the Gladstone bag over one arm and smiled. 'Please, let me help. Will your baby come to me?'

'Oh, thank you, but are you sure? You have your own bag and he's quite heavy.'

Sarah smiled. 'I can manage. He looks such a dear little chap.'

The baby's lower lip wobbled as his mother handed him over, but Sarah smiled at him and hummed a little tune, and he forgot to cry.

'You're good with him,' said the woman, a smile softening her haggard face. 'Do you have children of your own?'

'Sadly not.'

As they moved slowly down the gangway in the queue of passengers, Sarah Betts thought of Harry Delaney. She supposed they might have had children one day. After they'd dealt with Arthur Chiltern, and she was the grieving widow, she and Harry would have had enough money to live in any way they wanted. She felt a twinge of sadness. If only he hadn't lost his nerve and endangered their plans, the future might have been very different.

As things turned out, in the end, she'd had no choice but to kill Harry. The drinking had been getting worse, and then there were the drugs. He'd become a liability. One day, he would make a mistake and give them away.

She'd been angry when he failed the first time at the simple task of spiking Pashley's drink and stealing his cabin key. Harry had sulked and said it wasn't his fault, but she'd made sure he didn't dare let her down a second time. The next evening, he'd had Pashley's key in his hand when she came to the storeroom, and Pashley was barely conscious when she reached his cabin.

He too had left her no alternative. Arthur Chiltern had been far too big a prize to let a grubby journalist like Charles Pashley expose her past and ruin everything. Attempting to silence him with money, even if she'd had enough to succeed, would have been useless. What he gloried in was power over others. She smiled, recalling his vanity over the importance of his work. He'd liked to use words to destroy others. It was fitting that words had killed him.

Resting her cheek against the baby's damp, silky head, she observed the two policemen at the bottom of the gang-way. She had to get past them. Her heartbeat quickened. She forced herself to listen to what the baby's mother was saying; to smile and nod as if they were friends.

One of the policemen held up his hand and stopped the family just ahead of them. He made a great business of studying their papers. Fool, she thought. The woman's so plain. She couldn't possibly be mistaken for me.

It would be their turn next. Her fingernails found a plump fold in the baby's chubby arm and pinched it hard.

The baby let out a volley of screams, and the toddler clutched her mother's skirt and started to cry. As the baby's screams grew louder, he began to convulse. Scowling, the nearest policeman beckoned them forward. Sarah bowed her head and brought it close to the baby's, as if she was trying to comfort him. The policeman threw the briefest of glances at her passport then let her through. The mother followed with the toddler.

'I think he wants you,' said Sarah, handing the baby back.

People standing around them moved away until there was a space around the little party. 'The baby must be ill,' a woman muttered to her husband. 'You don't know where they've come from. Keep away.'

Unperturbed, Sarah ignored the hostile stares. 'Poor little thing,' she murmured, exuding concern. 'We should find a doctor straight away.'

The woman shook her head as she rocked the baby from side to side, desperately trying to soothe him. 'No, it will be too expensive. This happens often. He'll be calm soon.'

'Is someone meeting you?'

'Yes. We'll be alright. Thank you, you've been very kind.'

Sarah smiled sweetly. 'It was a pleasure. If there's nothing more I can do, I'll say goodbye.' She bent forward and patted the toddler's head, then, careful to act as if she was in no hurry, walked away. The baby had turned out to be an even better distraction than she had hoped.

Her heart leapt; she was free. And as she'd eaten nothing since last night, she was hungry. The first thing she was going to do was find some food.

* * *

De Silva squinted into the sun. It was impossible to watch every gangway. He hoped that these local policemen were good at their jobs.

'Is there any sign of her yet?' Jane appeared at his elbow.

'I don't think so, although I can't be sure. There's such a crowd leaving the ship. I hadn't expected there to be so many people.'

'After so long at sea, I expect most of the passengers would like to walk around on dry land for a few hours. They may not all be leaving the ship for good.'

For a few moments, they stood in silence, observing the policemen at the bottom of each gangway. They did look to be detaining some passengers, but it was hard to see the faces of the people they stopped. Presumably, they were satisfied they were harmless, for all of them were, eventually, allowed to go on their way.

De Silva began to fear the exercise was a waste of time. Perhaps Diana March, or as he now thought of her, Sarah Betts, was still hidden on the ship. It might be best to bring the local police on board to search for her.

He was about to tell Jane that he was going to find William Petrie and suggest a change of plan when there was a commotion at the bottom of one of the gangways. De

Silva and Jane saw that people were backing away from two women who had a toddler and a baby with them. The baby seemed to be ill. The taller of the two women was speaking to her friend.

Why did the little scene arouse his suspicions? De Silva couldn't explain, but it did. He looked around for one of the sailors with binoculars that William Petrie had promised to arrange, but they were nowhere to be seen.

'What is it?' asked Jane.

'The two women down there. The ones with the toddler and the baby who looks to be ill in some way. I think the taller one's her.'

The tall woman turned away and began to stroll in the direction of the exit from the dock. Despite the shabby coat she wore, she had an unmistakeable air of elegance.

He made up his mind. 'I'm going after her. Will you find Petrie for me? Tell him where I've gone. I'll try to round up a few of the policemen on the quayside to help me.'

CHAPTER 32

It was much harder to see what was happening on the level of the quayside than it had been up on deck. He moved through the crowd, trying to look in all directions, but there was no sign of her. The three policemen he had managed to round up at short notice fanned out to search too.

He had almost given up hope when he saw her among a group of men by a food stall. Pushing through the crowd, he stopped a few yards away. She was eating from a small bowl, dipping in a wedge of naan to scoop up the food. He took the last few steps and put his hand on her shoulder. 'Sarah Betts, you're under arrest.'

She swung round, her eyes wide. For a moment, she froze, then so fast that he didn't have time to duck, the bowl flew at him and curry splattered his face. He put up a hand to wipe the mess away and immediately regretted it when chilli burned his eyes. Tears streamed down his cheeks as he saw the back of the shabby brown coat whisk away into the crowds. Half blind, he couldn't follow.

'Water!' he shouted to the stallholder. 'Quickly!'

The man let out an indignant stream of words in a language de Silva didn't understand. 'Water!' he shouted again, frantically pantomiming washing his face. A grubby boy loitering nearby grinned at him. 'He says who will pay for the broken bowl.'

'To hell with his bowl. Find me some water.'

The boy led him to a nearby fountain and de Silva sluiced his eyes. He cursed under his breath: he had lost her.

'Did you see where that lady went?' he asked the boy, when he could see clearly again.

'Yes.'

'Show me.'

The boy looked at him expectantly.

'Oh, very well.'

De Silva fished in his pocket and found a few coins. The boy took them and scampered away.

'Hey! Where do you think you're going?'

The boy stopped and pointed towards the mouth of a narrow alley. 'This way.'

The dark alleys and sun-drenched courtyards they ran through reminded de Silva of the back streets of Colombo. There, he had known every inch of them, but here, it was a different matter. The boy darted along like quicksilver. Keeping up soon had de Silva puffing but to lose sight of his guide would be a disaster.

Women hanging out washing, children playing, and old men squatting in doorways smoking or chewing tobacco watched them curiously as they ran by. Their feet kicked up dust that made de Silva's nose and eyes itch. A dry, stale taste parched his mouth. His heart thudded, and his lungs felt as if they would burst.

Once or twice, the boy stopped to speak with someone before dashing on. De Silva assumed he was asking if they had seen a woman answering to Betts' description. At last, he halted so abruptly that de Silva nearly ran into the back of him. 'What is it?' he asked crossly, wiping sweat from his forehead. 'Why have you stopped?'

The boy put his finger to his lips and pointed to a house with a peeling, blue door. From the sign on the wall, it looked to be a lodging house. 'My friend says he saw the lady go in there, sahib.'

'Is he sure?'

The boy nodded. His skinny hand reached out and tugged at the pocket of de Silva's jacket. De Silva batted the hand away.

'Watch the door while I go in. If the lady comes out, follow her and get a message to me to tell me which way you went.'

The blue door creaked, and he stepped into a narrow, dark lobby. A sour-faced woman in a drab green robe eyed him suspiciously.

'Did a tall lady in a brown coat come in here? An English lady?'

The woman's lips stayed clamped shut. He pulled his badge out of his inside pocket. 'Police.'

She peered at the badge. De Silva was afraid it wouldn't mean anything to her, or she wouldn't understand him, but then she gave a reluctant nod. 'The third floor,' she said in a fractured accent. 'Number twelve.'

The stairs creaked under his feet as he hauled himself up a succession of steep flights. On each landing, there was a small window, but he doubted the panes of glass had been cleaned for a long time. The grime on them was so thick that light barely managed to penetrate. Where any persistent ray of sunshine did relieve the gloom, it danced with motes of dust.

On the third landing, de Silva paused to catch his breath. A door with the number twelve on it faced him. At a right angle, another stood ajar. He glimpsed a basin and a worn, enamelled bath inside.

Behind the door to room twelve, he heard someone move about. It must be Diana March. He had no gun. The best he could do now was try to surprise her and hope that, if she was armed, she wouldn't have time to reach for her weapon.

He was about to barge in when the door was opened for

him. A towel in her hand, Sarah Betts stared at him for a second then tried to slam the door in his face. He jammed his shoulder in the way then hurled himself after her as she dashed to the bed where the Gladstone bag and its contents were strewn across the counterpane. He caught her wrist before she had time to snatch up a small pistol, twisting her around to face him and dragging her back to the landing. She was stronger than he'd expected.

'You're under arrest,' he gasped. 'It will be better for you if you come quietly.'

'Oh, you'd like that, wouldn't you, Inspector? What a triumph for a provincial policeman. Inspector de Silva saves the day.'

He ignored the jibe. 'You do not have to say anything. But it may harm your—'

The bite was unexpected and so hard that he yelped and released her. Cradling his wounded hand, he ran after her in pursuit. Up the next flight they went, and the next, until there were no more stairs to climb, and a low door faced them.

Sunlight blinded him as he emerged into an aerial world of chimneys and water tanks, thrown into sharp relief by the scorching sun. When his eyes grew accustomed to the brightness, he saw her facing him.

'Give yourself up,' de Silva said calmly. 'We have the letter you wrote to Harry Delaney, and the dispatches you stole from Charles Pashley.'

'Forgeries. You must have planted them.'

'We also have a photograph of you with Harry Delaney in Bombay. How do you explain that?'

She lifted her chin. 'I have powerful people behind me. They'll expose your lies.'

'I wouldn't count on that. Be assured, you will have to answer for your crimes, and a man like Arthur Chiltern will shy away from being involved in a scandal. Give yourself up. You've nowhere left to run.'

She laughed, and the coldness in her eyes made his skin prickle.

'Oh, you're wrong there, Inspector.'

She glanced to her left where a narrow walkway ran along the edge of the roof of the next-door house. 'I have an excellent head for heights. Can you say the same?'

De Silva couldn't, although he was pleased to find that this airy world troubled him far less than usual. He took another step.

She moved onto the walkway. At intervals, metal poles stuck up from the adjoining house's roof, as if there had been a plan to build another storey onto the structure. A long moment passed, then she smiled. 'Goodbye, Inspector. I hope we never meet again.'

She turned and started to walk. De Silva thought of the boy waiting in the alley: unlikely to be a help now. He must force himself to follow her. Cautiously, he edged along, his heart beating faster as small pieces of masonry crumbled under his feet and ricocheted down to the courtyard far below. Each time he reached one of the metal poles, he paused a moment to steady his spinning head.

Suddenly, he heard a crack. Ahead, close to where she stood, a much larger piece of masonry had shifted from its position. As it rocked, dislodging its neighbours, she grabbed the nearest pole. It held firm, but her foothold had gone. Five floors below, sleepy cats basked in the sun. A man with a donkey and cart ambled across the courtyard, oblivious to the drama taking place high above him.

Slowly, Sarah Betts' fingers unclasped from the pole.

CHAPTER 33

De Silva stood at the window of their Cairo hotel room and watched dawn streak the sky. The street below him was already busy; he wondered if the city ever slept. He was glad it was morning. It might be some time before he stopped reliving in his dreams the moment when Sarah Betts had plummeted to her death.

Jane stirred. 'Come back to bed, dear. It's far too early to get up.'

He climbed under the sheet and put his arms around her.

'Are you still dreaming about her falling?' she asked.

'I'm afraid so, but it will pass. I'm determined to enjoy the rest of our holiday. I can see us getting a taste for this travelling business – the world will be our lobster.'

'Oyster, dear, as you know perfectly well,' said Jane with a smile.

He chuckled and kissed the top of her head. 'What would you like to do today?'

They had spent the first few days in Cairo quietly, often sat reading in the hotel's palm-shaded gardens. Between those times, they visited the cavernous national museum with its dusty cases of painted mummies, animal deities, and ancient treasures. They inspected a church and a mosque and wandered through markets pungent with the aroma of spices. In mazes of narrow streets, probably little changed since the time when the Romans built their fortress on the banks of the Nile, they watched goldsmiths and silversmiths working at their craft. They drank innumerable glasses of sweet tea and syrupy coffee. De Silva took pictures everywhere they went.

News came from William Petrie that after the verdict of not guilty in Sarah Betts' trial for the murder of her first husband, a detective at Scotland Yard, who had mistrusted the verdict, had kept an eye on her. His files showed that she and Harry Delaney started to be seen together six months later. At the time, Delaney was a nightclub singer, but there were rumours he had a criminal past. The detective lost track of the pair when they left England.

'I wonder if poor Arthur Chiltern was their first intended victim, or whether there were others between him and the murder of her first husband,' Jane mused when the story emerged.

'I doubt we'll ever find out. One thing's for sure, Chiltern had a lucky escape. I didn't take to the man, but I wouldn't wish a wife like Diana March on him.'

At breakfast in the hotel's pleasant dining room, they decided to make the trip out to the pyramids that day. 'If we're not too late to find a guide,' said de Silva.

'I'm sure we'll find someone to take us. Let's ask at reception.'

The hotel recommended a guide who was, they assured the de Silvas, excellent. His camels were also very docile.

'Camels?' De Silva's eyebrows shot up. He hadn't expected camels, but Jane seemed delighted with the idea, and he didn't want to disappoint her.

'People say you can even climb up the Great Pyramid of Cheops to see the view from the top and take tea,' said Jane brightly. She looked at de Silva and giggled. 'I was only joking, dear.'

'I'm glad to hear it. Camels will be quite enough to cope with.'

* * *

He enjoyed the first part of the expedition as their horse and cart jingled through the streets of Cairo. Streets that grew quieter and more countrified until the city ended somewhat abruptly in the desert. A small caravan of camels sat and waited in the shade of a grove of palm trees. De Silva observed the nearest one dubiously. Chewing its cud, it looked back at him with a supercilious expression. It knows I'm a novice, he thought.

'Camels are much misunderstood, you know,' remarked Jane, as if she had read his mind. 'If they're well treated, I'm told they're intelligent, friendly animals.' She nudged him. 'We must have a picture, dear, mustn't we?'

Suddenly, de Silva's interest in photography dwindled, but he took a picture of the camels all the same, then put the camera back in its case and settled the strap around his neck. He offered up a silent prayer to any deity who happened to be listening that his camel would be one of the well-treated variety.

Their guide had soon singled out the two beasts they were to ride. 'Very tame,' he said. 'Very nice.'

De Silva nodded, trying to show more confidence than he felt.

Helped by the camel driver, Jane mounted with admirable elegance. Then it was de Silva's turn. As instructed, he climbed into the saddle then leant back as the camel got up on its hind legs. When it was settled, it grunted and hauled itself up on its front legs. The camel driver indicated that de Silva should lean forward now and steady himself with the handhold at the front of the saddle.

The guide mounted, and they set off. The camel's hair felt coarse and scratchy to de Silva's touch. He was glad he wore western dress, with long trousers and thick socks. It was good that his animal did seem to be biddable too. After a while, he even started to enjoy its swaying gait. Perhaps this wasn't going to be so bad after all.

Small in the distance, the pyramids increased in size as they drew nearer. Bathed in the golden rays of the morning sun and guarded by the huge, lion-pawed Sphinx, they were a magnificent sight. Busy marvelling, de Silva suddenly noticed that his camel was getting behind the rest. He cast his mind back to the few occasions when he had ridden a horse in Nuala. How did you make them speed up? Squeeze with your legs – that was it.

Gently, he applied some pressure; the camel took no notice. He tried again, harder this time. The beast gave an angry grunt and jerked sideways, almost unseating him. Then its ears flattened, its rubbery lips peeled back from its yellowed teeth, and it set off at a gallop.

He just had time to glimpse Jane's shocked face as he flew past her, his camera bouncing against his chest in frantic concert with the thundering beat of his heart. With a mixture of exhilaration and alarm, he felt the wind stream into his face. It was one thing to make a camel go faster, but how did you stop it? He hoped he was going to get back to Nuala unscathed.

Then, as the pyramids filled his vision, the effort of hanging on banished all other thoughts from his mind. What a holiday this had turned out to be!